ENTICED BY A
CARTEL BOSS

A. GAVIN

Enticed by a Cartel Boss
Copyright 2019 by A. Gavin

Published by Mz. Lady P Presents

SYNOPSIS

Ani Nyleen Mack is your typical all-American girl. Until one day, she's not. In the blink of an eye, young Ani has to learn the ins and outs of the game to become the hottest thing the streets have ever seen. But trying to fill shoes way bigger than hers, both literally and figuratively, is harder than it looks and being caught up in her father's shadow has Ani doubting everything she thought she knew.

The field that Ani's in requires protection so when she meets Owen, her new bodyguard, it's a match made in heaven. He needs a job and she needs a protector. Sooner rather than later, their feelings get involved and before either of them realizes what they've done, they'll be taken on a whirlwind rollercoaster of passion, pain and redemption. With Owen by her side, Ani knows no boundaries, but will that do more harm than good in the end? And will Owen lose his morals behind the enticement of a cartel boss?

🜲 I 🜲

ANI (A-NEE) MACK

I sat in the back of the courtroom with my shades covering my tear stained eyes. The judge had just handed his sentence down. How could I be crying over someone that I'd never even met before? Nonetheless, he was a part of me. At the end of the day, it was his blood was pumping through my veins.

The court officers helped him stand up and began to escort him away. As fate would have it, he looked my way, and our eyes connected. For a brief moment, the world around us had stopped. The man who helped make me was staring at me as if he had just seen a ghost. Then a sinister smile formed on his face. He nodded at me and then winked his eye as the officers lead him to the back.

Kindred Edwards looked like everything I had dreamed of. We were damn near identical, and he'd be a fool to deny me. I had inherited his hot chocolate colored skin. His natural black hair was cut into a low fade with sprinkles of gray. His youthful face gave me slight hope that I would age gracefully when I reached his age. Admiring him was one thing, but I still had uncertainty in my heart about him.

Six a months ago, my mother informed me, after many years of asking, who my father was. The only reason she decided to tell me was because she knew this day was coming. I'm not sure why she held this information from me, but I'm starting to see that it was for the best. My emotions were at an all-time high, but the only problem was I didn't know how exactly to feel. I didn't know whether to be sad, mad or just plain fed up. One thing for certain, I wasn't going to shed a tear. My mother instilled in me, at an early age, to never cry over things you cannot change. I couldn't change the fact that he didn't want to raise me, and honestly, I had grown to be okay with the decision he made.

I made my way out of the courtroom doors and stepped into the fresh air. The Chicago summer's sun beamed down on me as I closed my eyes and took deep breaths. In my six-inch heels, I ran across the street to my car, not sure what prompted me to wear these shoes or this outfit. The black leather pencil skirt was cutting off my circulation, and the flowing blouse was far too much for my taste. However, I was determined to look my best. I wasn't going to look like the hot struggle mess that was currently my life. He was going to take one look at me and see that my mother had done a great job raising me, without him.

As soon as I sat down in the car, I placed my hair into a bun, kicked the heels off, and replaced them with my slides. This skirt was so tight that it was checking my blood pressure and I needed out of it, quickly. I unzipped it and slid it out from under me. A knock on my window caused me to grab my chest in fear, but then I screamed out when I realized that my lower body was exposed. The man turned around, placed his hand over his eyes, and kept saying how sorry he was. I was able to grab my joggers and throw them on.

"I'm done now. Who are you and why are you knocking on my window?"

"My name's Tony and this is Ziggy. Kindred sent us here. We have a message for you."

Why did he have a message for me? He hasn't sent a message in twenty-four years, so why now? I needed to get the hell out of here and away from all things Kindred Edwards. Not wasting any time, I turned the engine over on my car. Low and behold, it wouldn't start. I've been meaning to get it looked at, but with my busy schedule, I just didn't have the time to do it.

"This is how all horror movies start, Tony. I'm sure you and Ziggy are fine gentlemen, but I'm gonna need you to step away from my car before I mace you. I'm almost certain that you have the wrong person!" I yelled out with a broken voice.

My hands trembled as I continued to turn the engine over. If I could kick my own ass, I would. My mom told me, more times than I care to admit to get this car checked.

"No, I'm sure I have the right person. Ani Nyleen Mack, I was sent to talk to you by your father, Kindred Edwards." His name rolled off his tongue like it was nothing, but it cut through me like a knife.

"H-he doesn't have shit to say to me. Now if you'll excuse me, I have business to tend to. You gentleman have a blessed day. Oh, and you can tell Mr. Edwards to kiss my ass and don't send anyone after me!"

I don't know who he thinks he is, but we had nothing to speak about. He made his decision, twenty-four years ago when he decided that being a father wasn't something he wanted to do. My mother and I were just fine without him.

Finally, my engine turned over, and I sped off leaving them in the dust. I didn't have anything to say to them, and they didn't have anything to say to me. I needed to speak to my mom and get some of this stuff cleared up. It was time for her to finally tell me everything. Kindred wasn't a normal man, and I needed to know if my life was going to change with him behind bars.

2

MARIYAH MACK

"Ma! Ma, where you at? I need to talk to you!" Ani's voice echoed through the house. She had just returned home from the courthouse, and I knew that she had a million and one questions.

Speaking on Kindred wasn't something that I was interested in, but I knew that Ani needed to know everything. Her life was about to change, and she needed to be prepared. A few minutes later, she came bursting into my office breathing hard with a tear-stained face.

"Did you know?" she asked while she tried to catch her breath.

"Did I know what?"

"Did you know that my father has been living in Chicago for years?" She studied my face to find her answer.

"Yes."

"Why didn't you tell me? Don't you think that's something that I should have known? All this time you knew he was right here in this city, but you kept that information from me. Why would you do that? What kind of mother keeps her child away from their father? This is ridiculous, ma. I don't know if I can get past this. This kind of betrayal is the worst."

This is where I had to stop her. Every decision that I made involving Kindred was to protect Ani in every way possible.

"Watch how you talk to me, Ani'Yah! I understand that you're upset and that you have a lot of questions to ask, but you will not disrespect me. Everything that I've ever done was to protect you. Do you have any clue who your father is and what he does for a living? I think you need to start there before you go questioning my decisions as a parent."

I hated raising my voice at her, but I could not allow her to disrespect the decisions that I made twenty-two years ago in order to protect her. She plopped down in the chair in front of my desk, and I handed her an iPad.

"Calm down and read over this. Hopefully, this will answer some of the questions that you have. Once you're done, let me know, and we can have a civil conversation like adults. I'll be back."

My phone had been ringing for the past five minutes, and I knew that the process had begun.

"Hello Tony," I answered. "It's been a while since I've heard from you. What can I help you with?"

"You know why I'm calling, Mariyah. It's time."

I hung up the phone, closed my eyes, and took a deep breath. I hadn't prepared myself for this, but there was no turning back, and I needed to get it together for Ani's sake. She was going to need my strength throughout this process even though I wasn't mentally ready for these next steps.

"Ma, can we talk?" she spoke up.

"Of course, give me a few minutes, and I'll be right in."

For years, I contemplated telling her everything she needed to know. My child was a gentle soul and when she found out what I was, hiding it was going to take a lot of love and care to keep her from falling into a deep, dark hole. I didn't want this to affect her life at an early age, so I made the conscious decision to withhold valuable information. There was only a matter of time before Kindred's terrible decisions caught up with him and brought to light the very thing that I was trying to hide.

After gathering my thoughts, I returned to my office to face a confused and scared Ani. I wanted to see if she was going to say some-thing, but she sat with a dumbfounded look on her face. The informa-tion on the iPad had her in shock, and I would expect nothing less. It's not every day that you find out that your father is one of the most ruthless cartel bosses within the United States.

Yes, Kindred Edwards is head of *the* Edwards Cartel. The Edwards Cartel is responsible for bringing in about seventy-five percent of the nation's finest cocaine. They were ruthless and feared globally. Many tried to imitate and duplicate, but none were successful. Kindred and his brother ran the family business with an iron fist when their father retired.

Nevertheless, like all great stories, they end with death and dishon-esty. After his brother was killed, Kindred was left to take care of everything. To the streets, he was known as Big Kin, but to me, he was Kindred, the kind-hearted, loving, and devoted boyfriend.

"Mom," Ani sobbed as she called out to me. "What's going on? What did I just read?"

"Ani, I know it's a lot to take in, and it'll be even harder to accept, but hopefully, with time, things will get better. Unfortunately, for now, your life is about to get a little more complicated. I'll start from the beginning and explain everything you need to know. Feel free to stop me, if needed.

"Your father and I met when I was eighteen years old and living in California. It was love at first sight. He was smart, kind-hearted, and loving. My parents hated him due to his reputation, but I loved him through thick and thin. When we met, he hadn't taken over the family business, and I knew nothing about it. I heard buzz through the streets about it, but he shielded me from that.

That is until Kendrell was killed. He was killed the night of my twenty-first birthday party. I remember that day like it was yesterday because that's the same day that I found out that I was pregnant with you. There was so much going on that night that I didn't even get a chance to tell Kindred the good news. In the middle of my party, Kindred received the news about his brother, and I was rushed out of the club and taken back to his house. That's when I found out that the rumors were true. I thought that I had been to his house before, but I was sadly mistaken when I was taken to a mansion on the outskirts of the city. I begged Kindred to tell me what he was about to do, but he wouldn't answer me. He had zoned out and wasn't paying me any attention. I don't know what he did that night, but from that day forward, Kindred was a completely different person.

Let's fast forward to Kendrell's funeral. On the day of the funeral, I was all dressed and ready to go. The trucks were due to arrive shortly, and I'd be joining the rest of the family. When I came downstairs, Kindred ordered me to stay back, and it was non-negotiable. I cried all day because, for the life of me, I couldn't understand why I couldn't go. When he returned home that night, he explained everything to me. I soon found out that he was now the head of the Edwards Cartel and whoever killed Kendrell was watching. He needed us safe until they found out who was after them. He knew that I was pregnant with you without me telling him.

We're gonna fast forward again. Two years later, Kindred's name was big, and he was deeper in the business than he'd ever been. Money was coming in by the boatloads, and I had free range to do whatever I wanted. That is until our lives were almost taken at a grocery store. The glitz and glam had blinded me and almost made me forget that I had a child to live for. We had a child to live for. I tried day in and day out to explain this to Kindred, but he was too far gone. After much deliberation with myself, I made the conscious decision to pack up my things and leave. You having a normal and safe childhood was all that I cared about. I took all the money that I had saved up and went came to Chicago. I figured since Chicago is such a big city, we'd blend right in.

He was so caught up in this mess that he didn't even realize that we were gone. He tried to reach out to me many times, but he eventually gave up. Tony, the man that you met earlier, was like a big brother to me and continued looking out for us. He would send money every month, birthday cards every year, and presents for Christmas."

I reached in my desk drawer, pulled out a folder, and handed it to her. She quickly opened it and began reading the documents. The folder contained bank statements dating back twenty-two years ago. It was never touched, and it held well over twenty million dollars.

When Ani read the last page, her eyes grew wide, and her mouth fell open. She was the sole owner of this bank account, and everything in it belonged to her. I decided that she wouldn't have access to this account until she knew exactly where she came from. I knew that I wasn't going to be able to explain that amount of money to her before this day. I do pretty well for myself right now, but not that damn well.

"Ani, there's more," I said as she continued to scan the documents.

When she heard that, her head shot up and she gave me a confused look. As I said, there's a lot for me to explain. Things were about to get real for her, and it was either sink or swim.

"There's more? What more could you possibly have to tell me? I'm the daughter of a damn cartel boss, and I didn't even know it! I've been walking around here day in and day out just living my life like a normal girl when I'm far from that. Nothing about this is normal, mom!" she yelled out in frustration and fear.

Her outburst is the exact reason why I left that life alone. My daughter was a soft, loving person, and I knew that this life would be too much for her to handle.

"I'm sorry, sweetie, but yes, there's more. Even though Kindred is behind bars, the business must still go on. This is a twenty-four hours, seven days a week, three hundred and sixty-five days a year kind of business and the show must go on. Per the family guidelines, the business is handed to the next living child. Kindred didn't have any additional children outside of you—"

"Stop, no. You are not about to say what I think you are going to say. Lies, all lies, every last one of them. Call me when you've got your head on straight. This is too much. I refuse to sit here and believe that you're about to tell me that I'm in charge of a fuckin' cartel because I'm Kindred's only child. Hell no!"

She got up from the chair and took off running out of the door. I went behind her, but I wasn't quick enough. She started up her car and sped out of the driveway. This is exactly what I was afraid of.

"Hey Tony, I tried explaining everything to her, but she took off. Watch out for her, please. If I know my child, then I know she's going to Britton's gym. It's off 22nd Street and Canalport Avenue. Please so make sure that she's safe and she's okay, but don't approach her. We need to get a new detail on her."

"It's already in the works. Hey, Riyah, thanks for taking my call. I know how hard it's been for you, and I'm sorry for not doing more. You know Kind—"

"Don't do that, Tony. It's not your fault, so there's no need for you to apologize. Just take care of her. I'm a big girl, and I can take care of myself."

We hung up, and I prayed for Ani's peace of mind. Things were about to get realer than real.

3

ANI MACK

My mind was racing as I left the house. How was someone supposed to react to this kind of news? I woke up this morning planning to see my father for the first time. I did not plan on finding out that I was going to have to step up and run a whole cartel. What makes them think that I'm cut out for this? I know nothing about this life. My life was just fine the way it was.

When I arrived at Britton's gym, I hopped out and ran right in. It's Tuesday afternoon, and she didn't have any clients. I had her calendar, so you best believe that I checked. Her undivided attention was needed right now!

"Hey Ani, what's good?" her receptionist Paisley spoke to me, but I ran right past her towards the office. I didn't mean to be rude, but this was serious, and I needed advice.

"Brit, you in here?"

"Yeah babe, I'm in the bathroom. Give me just a second!"

I plopped on the plush couch she had in her office and curled up in a ball. This day was way too much for me to deal with on my own, and the only person that would understand how I was feeling was Britton. I've known her for a short period of time, but we clicked immediately, and she was the sister that I never had. She knew just what to say anytime I needed her. No judgments were made, and she kept things one hundred with me.

"Aw, what's wrong? Who broke my Ani's heart today?" she asked while leaning against her desk.

"You're gonna wanna sit down for this."

She raised her eyebrow in curiosity but didn't say anything. Instead, she removed my legs from the couch and sat next to me.

"Tell me what's going on. It's gotta be serious if you're telling me to sit down and you're curled up on my couch like a baby."

"It's bad, Brit, really bad."

"Girl, stop being dramatic and tell me what's going on."

I sat up and started telling her everything that happened today. By the time I was finished, Britton just had a blank stare on her face. I waved my hand in front of her face, and she didn't flinch.

"Bitch, you're about to be the next Griselda Blanco! You're gonna be running a whole fuckin' cartel. Wow. Just wow. I'm genuinely shocked." I wasn't expecting that reaction from her. I expected her to be just as shocked and confused as me.

"Brit, that ain't what I need from you right now. What am I gonna do?"

"What do you want to do? It's all about how you feel. Don't make any decisions without knowing every single detail. You'll be able to make a calculated decision once you know everything there is to know about this business."

She was right. I couldn't go into this situation without knowing any and everything. This wasn't a job to take lightly, and I'll be damned if I just said yes and got myself into a world of charges and jail time. Obviously, Kindred made some mistakes, and that's what got him locked up. I needed to know exactly what mistakes he made and how he made them.

"Do you have to make a decision right now?" Brit inquired even though she already knew the answer to that.

"Yeah, I was actually just talking to mom about it and took off running when she started going down the hill with it. God, I need a drink." My melodramatic attitude caused Britton to roll her eyes, but I didn't care. I was allowed to be dramatic right now. This shit wasn't normal by far. This was next level shit.

"Well, today is your lucky day. I'm done for the day, and I'm hungry. Let's get out of here and relax a little, my treat." She flashed her perfect smile my way and dragged me off the couch and out the door.

"Paisley, hold all of my calls. If it's an emergency, then just transfer it to my cell."

"Yes, ma'am. Oh, before you go, Range paid for sixteen sessions with you. He spared no expense and paid the ridiculous amount that I quoted him, up front. I'm sorry Britton, but he's got it bad for you. Also, I'd like my commission paid out via a new Chanel bag."

Brit dropped her purse on the coffee table and began massaging her temples.

"Oh God, sixteen sessions with his ass is gonna make me commit felony murder."

Range was a man that got whatever he wanted whenever he wanted it, except for Britton Matthews. He is a high-priced lawyer here in the city and is stopping at nothing to have her on his arm. He had it bad for her, and it was honestly hard to watch. It's not that he wasn't every woman's dream. It's just that he's not Britton's dream. She wasn't the type to have a "type", but she just wanted someone real and down to earth, someone that was going to go the distance with her and make her happy. Range wasn't that. He was too egotistical and demanding. It wasn't going to work well with her attitude.

"Don't even trip, Brit. If you want, I can be here during his sessions. That way you aren't entirely alone with him," I offered up the help, and I'm sure she was going to take it.

"That would be amazing, Ani! Thank you so much. What would I do without you?" she screeched as she grabbed her keys and walked to the garage.

"You'd be committing murder if I wasn't around. We can't have that. Jail isn't like *Orange is the New Black*, at all." We both fell out laughing as we slid in her car and went to lunch.

My day wasn't over by far, but for now, I wasn't going to dwell on the decision that needed to be made. When my mom asked me again, I was going to have an answer along with some questions. For now, I was going to enjoy this lunch date with my best friend. The sun was still out, and the temperature was warm. I placed my shade on my face and closed my eyes. The sun was beaming down on me and giving me life.

We cruised for a little while, and I wondered what we were going to eat. The car came to a stop, and when I opened my eyes, I noticed that we were at my apartment building. I didn't know why we were here because I thought we were on our way to lunch.

"Why are we here?" I asked as Brit pressed the garage opener and sped to her spot. She parked, took off her seatbelt, and turned towards me.

"I love you Ani, I really do, but I'll be damned if I'm seen out in public with you and this tired outfit. Let's get you changed, and then we can go eat."

I wanted to protest because what I was in was comfortable, but then again, she was right. I couldn't be seen like this.

"Come on, lil girl." We made it into my apartment, and I quickly searched for something to put on.

"Tell me more about this whole cartel business. This isn't something that happens every day, so I need all the tea. Are there fine ass men involved because baby, a bitch is in NEED!" she yelled out as she plopped down on the bed.

"I don't know yet. I haven't even decided if I'm going to do it. You know that my life will drastically change if I commit to this. No more unscheduled lunch dates, no more coming to your rescue at the gym, or drunken nights at the club. Are *you* ready for that change?"

This was going to be hard for both of us because we were as thick as thieves. We did everything together, and that was going to change *if* I took on this role. However, I wasn't one hundred percent sold. Too many questions were left unanswered.

I had finally picked out an outfit and walked out of the closet, only to see Brit all in my phone. She knew the passcode to it, so that wasn't really a shocker. My main concern was the fact that she was typing away fast as hell. There was no reason for her to be typing on that fast unless she had something to hide. I cleared my throat, and her eyes shot up.

"Whatcha doin', lil mama?"

She dropped the phone and took off running into the other room. I had no idea what she'd done, but I'm sure that it was about to piss me off. I picked up the phone and took a deep breath. My eyes scanned everything she typed, and it was as if the air left my body. I was going to kill her.

"Britton Lyle Matthews! I'm gonna fuckin' kill you! Where are you?" I yelled as I searched each room in my two-bedroom, two bathroom apartment. She had no idea what she had just done.

It took me ten minutes to find her, and when I did, her ass was hiding under my kitchen sink like a little ass kid. Tears were streaming down her eyes from laughter, but I didn't find any of this shit funny. She had lost her damn mind, but I was gonna help her find it in less than two seconds.

"Before you go off, just know that I'm doing this for you. You live a boring and normal life Ani. It's time to spice things up. I only set up a meeting for you to hear everything out. You have a ton of questions, and that's the only way that you're going to get the answers to them. I'll be with you every step of the way, and you know my guns bang if they're on some funny shit. Now come on, a bitch is hungry, and we're gonna need that drink. You have a meeting set up tonight with Tony."

Angry was an understatement. I was frustrated, agitated, and confused. I didn't know what to think, but at this point, there was no backing down. I grabbed my purse and headed out the door.

❧ 4 ❧

OWEN PIERCE

When my pops hit me up about a new gig that he had secured for me, I wasn't too thrilled. I made decent money at my current job, but he felt that it wasn't enough. He wanted me not to have to worry about a thing, and I appreciated that. However, my pride wasn't going to deal with this well. I can provide for myself and didn't want to keep taking daddy's hand-outs. The day I walked out of the jailhouse gates, I made a promise to myself that I wasn't going to do things the same way because I refused to go back.

"Baby, what's going on? You seem so distant. Is everything okay?" Camille stroked my chin with her tiny manicured finger as she laid on my chest.

"I'm good."

She raised her eyebrow as if she didn't think I was telling the truth.

"Tell me what's on your mind. I can't help you if I don't know what's going on with you, Owen."

She was now sitting up on her elbows waiting for me to explain things to her. I don't know what she expected out of me. She's fully aware that I'm not one to discuss my feelings. If I was going through some shit, then I was gonna handle it on my own.

"I'm good, shorty. I start a new gig today, and it's gonna take up a lot of my time." Against my better judgment, I decided to take the job in hopes that it would help put my life back on track.

This wasn't the life that I was supposed to be living. I wasn't supposed to be a convicted felon, and I damn sure wasn't supposed to serve a bid. I hated that I ended up being in the wrong place at the wrong time. I threw the cover off me and headed to the shower. I was supposed to meet Tony in a few hours, and he was gonna explain to me what the job entailed. Everything in me was telling me to stay at the car wash, but I couldn't pass up the amount of money he quoted.

Seven years ago, I got hit with a robbery charge. Even though I was an innocent bystander, the store clerk believed that all black men looked alike and swore that I was involved with it. The police hauled my ass off, and I plead guilty because I had a public defender who couldn't even remember my damn name.

I heard her open the shower door before I felt her tiny hands against my chest and her perky breasts caressed my back. Camille was everything that a man could want or need in life. It's just that she wasn't right for me. Shorty came from wealth and couldn't understand struggle even if it came and slapped her in the face. She tried to empathize with me and my situation, but I couldn't provide her the life that she had been accustomed to. Her father offered several times to help me with employment, but again, my pride wouldn't let me take it. If I let him help me, then I would forever be in debt to him. I refused to have that on my conscience.

She stood in front of me and looked at me with water dancing on the bottom of her amber colored eyes. Her full pink lips were poked out in a pout, and I knew that shit was about to go left.

"I feel like I'm losing you, Owen." The tears started falling down her face and mixing in with the shower water. She had no reason to believe that she was losing me and that was just her paranoia talking.

"You not."

"See, this is what I mean. You keep things short and push me away only when I'm trying to help you. Baby, this is a relationship, and we're in this together. I want to build with you and grow old with you. Why won't you let me in?"

"You're good. I'm here."

I didn't mean to come off cold, but I wasn't focused on any of that shit right now. My main focus was to get this money and live comfortably the way that I saw fit. Marriage, kids, and growing old was the furthest thing from my mind.

"Owen, you're stressed. Let me help ease things a little before you go on about your day."

Camille was a beautiful woman. Her tall, tan modelesque body could bring any man to their knees, and she knew it. She was gonna try to use her good looks and sex to get her way with me. That's why I didn't press her like that. I didn't need or like a woman that knew how fine she was and used it to her advantage. This song and dance was normal for us, and it had gotten old real quick.

Her body began moving down to the shower floor slowly, and her tiny hands used my chest for support. The feeling of her lips on my skin caused a tremble in my body, but it quickly went away. I grabbed her wrist and picked her body back up.

"Stop."

When she heard that word, you would have thought the devil was coming to pay us a visit.

"Who is she? Who's the woman that's taken you away from me? Owen, I know you, and I know you love when I please you. Why aren't you letting me do that?" She snatched her wrists out of my hand and started banging them against my chest.

"Shorty, chill. I'm not in the mood to fight with you. Your insecurities are showing." I stepped out of the shower and grabbed a towel.

"Owen, don't walk away from me! Tell me who she is!" She continued to yell and scream as I got dressed.

I wasn't in the business of putting my hands on women, but if she hit me again, then I was going to shake the shit out of her. Camille was putting on a show as she fell to the floor on her knees. Tears streamed out of her eyes as she folded herself into a ball.

"I'm out!" I yelled out as I walked down the stairs of her apartment and out of the door.

☙ 5 ❧

ANI MACK

The sun was still shining brightly as Britton, and I made it to a cute little spot tucked away in downtown. We'd been sitting outside on the patio for less than half an hour, and things were good, except for the fact that I was lost in my own thoughts. When Brit sent that text off to my mom explaining to her that I would have a sit down with Tony and the rest of Kindred's crew, I wanted to have a heart attack. There were so many questions that I wanted to ask about the man that abandoned me, but this isn't that way that I wanted to go about them.

For as long as I can remember, my mother was the only person there for me. She hustled hard day in and day out to cover everything that I needed. I may not have had everything I wanted, yet, somehow, she made a way out of no way to get everything I needed. There were times where I wanted to ask her who my father was, and why wasn't he helping us, but I didn't want to upset her. There were plenty of times where I would hear her crying at night asking God why this man would put her in this position even though she loved him so much. Every night I would pray for God to heal my mother and her broken heart. She was in love with this man, and I hope that they could eventually make it work. As far as our relationship, I wasn't so sure that we'd be good.

Britton pulled me out of my thoughts as she snapped her fingers in my face.

"It's going to be okay, Ani. I'll be with you every step of the way. Don't even worry about it. We're going in to see what they have to say. It's not like you have to make a decision right away. If it's something that you don't want to do, then we won't do it, and we can walk away and go back to our normal lives. You can continue working at the library, and I'll continue as a trainer."

Britton always made it seem like working at the library was a bad thing, but to know me is to love me. I was a lover of books, and I couldn't escape it even if I wanted to. One thing that I absolutely needed in my life was my own personal library.

"Get out of your head, Ani. Everything's going to be okay. I promise," she tried to reassure me, but I wasn't sold on it. Who in their right mind has to choose between having a normal life and running a male-dominated business?

We continued to talk and eat, but there was an uneasy feeling in my soul that caused me to search my surroundings. Something wasn't right, and I needed to figure it out. I didn't want to scare her, but I think someone was watching us. If Britton found out what was going on, then she would freak out and start busting her guns. Britton was no stranger to the streets, but that's a story for another day. For now, we needed to get out of here.

"Let's get out of here. I think I'm ready to face my mom. Will you come with me?"

She looked at me with her wide ice blue eyes. "Of course, I'll come with you. We drove my car anyway. How'd you expect to get there?" We engaged in a laugh and paid the waiter.

My mother lived in the Beverly neighborhood on Chicago's Southside. The drive wasn't close, but it wasn't as long as most. During the ride, that uneasy feeling was still there. Everything in me wanted to ignore it since I had too many other things on my mind, but I couldn't. It lingered over me, and it was time to turn around and see if someone was following us. Low and behold, there was a black SUV bobbing and weaving out of traffic. I didn't want to alarm Britton, but she was the driver, and she needed to know.

"Take a left at the stop light ahead."

She looked at me out the corner of her eye and did what I said. "Any particular reason that you're taking me on a completely different route to the house?"

"No, just drive."

The car was still following us, and panic started to settle in my heart. I didn't know what to do at this point. The sound of a phone ringing caused me to jump out of my skin.

My face flushed when I answered it. "Put the phone on speaker."

"Who is this?" I asked.

"Do as I say so that you can lose that car, Ani. Now, tell your friend to turn right at the end when you get to the small break in the road. You'll find yourself going through the Forest Preserves. When you get to the end of the trail make another right and stop on the west side of the train tracks. Do it quickly. You need to make it there before the next train comes. Let's go."

Against my better judgment, Britton stepped on the gas and did exactly what the caller instructed. I could see the train tracks about twenty yards in front of us, but I could also hear the train horn approaching.

Fear etched my face as I watched Britton speed down the road. "We're gonna be good Ani. Relax!" Shots rang out behind us as my heart damn near beat out of my chest. This is not how day one was supposed to go.

Britton was handling this like a pro. She was determined to get over those tracks. I, on the other hand, wasn't so sure that we were going to make it. My heart was about to hop out of my chest as we approached the tracks. The trains headlights were drawing near, and I just knew that I was about to meet my maker. I closed my eyes tightly as the car came to a screeching halt.

I went to scream but my mouth was covered, and my body was thrown into the back of another car. Things were happening so fast. I wasn't able to grasp what was taking place. The screeching of the tires informed me that I was being kidnapped. This is exactly why I don't want to be involved with this life.

"Britton where you at? Are you okay?" I yelled at the top of my lungs. I waited for an answer that never came. What the hell just happened? Who the hell was following me?

Calm down, Ani. This is a test. This is all a test.

I repeated this to myself over and over. That's when I realized that my eyes were still shut tight. I opened them and saw that I was laying across the back seat.

"Have you calm down yet, Ms. Ani?" I looked at the driver, and it was Tony. How did he know that I was being followed?

He looked at me in the mirror and raised his eyebrow. "Now you see why I told you to come with me? You're now a target and need to be protected at all times, Ani."

We continued on our way to my mother's house. No words were said for the remainder of the way. Honestly, I was too shaken up to say anything.

I noticed that Britton wasn't in the car, and I immediately feared the worst. "She's okay, Ani. She's in the car behind us with Ziggy. Relax."

When we arrived at my mother's house, I hopped out quickly and ran inside to find her. I need to know that she was safe. This was far too much for me to deal with and my anxiety was on the verge of giving me a heart attack.

"Mama! Where you at? Are you okay?" I yelled while running through the house like a chicken with my head cut off.

When I reached her office, she was leaning against the desk with her phone up to her ear. She disconnected the call when I walked up to her and wrapped my arms around her.

"Ani, why are you yelling through my house like you've lost your damn mind? What's the problem?"

My heart was in my throat, and it was hard for me to talk. "I-I can't do this ma. This is too much. I got people chasing me and shit. Brit and I almost got hit by a train mama..."

She looked at me with a blank expression on her face, and I had no idea what was going through her head.

"Now do you see why I didn't want you running out of here? This is a dangerous game Ani, and the minute you showed your face at Kindred's sentencing was the minute that you exposed yourself to the enemy. Have a seat for a minute and let me talk to Tony. I believe he has a detail for you. I'll be back to talk to you about your decision."

She switched out of the room with elegance and grace mixed with a face full of fear.

6

MARIYAH MACK

Hearing Ani explain what happened today shook me to the core. Chaos was already knocking at my doorstep. Ani had no idea how deep this game ran, and it was time for her to step up whether she liked it or not. Earlier after Ani left, I was informed that word had already hit the streets that the legendary Big Kin had a little girl taking over his territory while he completed his bid. This was now a serious matter. Ani now had a bright red target on her back. It was my job as her mother to protect her and unfortunately, the only way I saw that happening was to teach her everything that I knew about this game and hope that she would be able to come out on top.

I reached the living room and saw that Tony was finishing up a phone call. He turned towards me, and a hint of sorrow flashed in his eyes. Tony knew better than anyone that this was realer than real and there was no turning back.

He walked up to me and shook his head. I backed away from his tall overpowering frame and shook my head. Tears threatened to fall from my eyes as my hands trembled. Breath was caught in my throat, and I felt as if I was suffocating.

"This can't be happening Tony. Not my baby. This isn't what I wanted for her."

"I know, Riyah. Believe it or not Kin didn't want this for her either." He caught me before I backed into the table. "He sent a message for you. You know I gotta give it to you, Riyah."

He reached in his suit jacket and pulled out a piece of paper. The words on the paper tore through my heart. This was too much for one day. I balled the paper up and threw it in the trash. Tears streamed down my face threatening to expose my inner feelings. Kindred was the love of my life, and I never wanted to leave him alone. It's just that this game isn't for the weak, and it isn't for anyone with a family. It'll suck you in and turn you into a money hungry heathen.

The phone ringing in my pocket caused me to straighten up. "Hel-lo?" My voice croaked, and I hated that my emotions were on my sleeve. Whoever was at the end of the call could hear the emotion in my throat.

"You have a collect call from—"

The phone slipped out of my hand, and my eyes grew wide. How in the hell did he get my number? Tony wasted no time picking up the phone and accepting the charges. I didn't need to speak to him. At this point, his only concern should have been his daughter. She's entered the game and was going to need all the advice she could get.

Tony and Kindred shared a few words with each other before he held the phone my way. "Just hear him out, Riyah."

Shaking my head, I walked away to find Ani. With his arm wrapped around my wrist, Tony pulled me back and placed the phone near my ear. "Hear him out, Mariyah. Please?"

The sigh that left my breath was enough to get him talking. His deep baritone voice removed any thought of me running away from this call. The voice that I had fallen in love with at the age of eighteen had set the butterflies off in my stomach. I hated to admit it, but not a soul on this earth could admit that they had my love like Kindred Amil Edwards. He was my most epic love story.

I cleared my throat and forced out, "Y-yes, Kindred?"

"Mariyah, damn, you sound good. However, I don't have much time to bask in that. There are a few things that you all need to do in order to ensure Ani'Yah's safety—"

Before he could get out another word, I corrected him. "She goes by Ani."

"Cool, I like that better. Tony has keys and codes to a place that I had built for y'all a long time ago. It's the safest place for you all to be right now. All the information that you need will be available to you when you get there. Leave now and don't look back. I gotta go but answer this fuckin' phone when I call, Mariyah!"

My eyes bucked at his audacity. Who the hell did Kindred think he was? Calling me and demanding something to *me*.

"Ma," Ani's voice was the only thing that could snap me out of the attitude that had formed.

Her appearance and demeanor had changed. My worst fear was coming true. She was about to tell me that she was ready. Everything in me was screaming that she wasn't, but at the end of the day, I had to trust that I raised her strong.

Again, my thoughts were interrupted by the sound of Tony's voice. "We have to get you guys out of here. I have to meet with the new detail. Ziggy's going to get you guys there, and then I'll meet up with you."

He placed a set of keys in my purse along with a piece of paper. "Those are the codes to the gates and the security system. I'll see y'all soon."

❧ 7 ❧

OWEN PIERCE

A presence behind me caused me to turn around with uncertainty. Thankfully, it was Tony walking towards me. A look of worry etched his face. His brows were pinched together, forming a mean scowl. There was only one direction that this conversation could go. He was gonna tell me that the job was no longer available.

"Hey, Owen. You're still interested in the job?" I hit him with a nod. "Cool, we have to get going right now. I'll explain what everything in the car. Leave your car here, and I'll have someone pick it up. Training starts now."

He started running towards a black SUV, and I jogged lightly behind him. We hopped in, and they sped off. Someone needed to start talking and telling me what was going on.

"What's going on, and what did I get myself into?" If I didn't ask now, then there would probably be no turning back.

"Your dad didn't explain what this was?"

"Nah."

Tony took in a deep breath and exaggerated when releasing it. His mouth opened, and he quickly explained only what I needed to know. It was my job to protect a woman by the name of Ani at all costs. She was never to leave my side. He wouldn't go into to detail about who she was. At the end of the day, she was an important person, and that's all that mattered.

"You gotta lady, Owen?" he asked as he bobbed and weaved outta traffic.

This was strictly business, and he didn't need to know about my life.

"Nah."

"Cool, this job doesn't allow love. It's an around the clock type of deal, but you will have two off days a week." He continued spittin' info about the job, but I was ready to get in and make money.

"Remember what I said. Keep shit professional for now. I'll introduce you to everyone, and then we'll get you taken care of." The calm outside of the house had nothing against the mood that was inside.

"Ani, calm your ass down! This isn't the fuckin' end of the world! What would Beyoncé do?"

"Matthew Knowles would never allow his daughter to do this, Britton! It's apples and fuckin oranges!"

The scared chick was pacing back and forth in a frenzy with her wild and curly hair following suit. There was obviously a lot going on at this moment. I took a step back and continued to let everything unfold. It wasn't my place to interfere.

"Who the hell is this?" A short chick with a cornbread fed body walked up to me and pointed her finger in my face.

Her eyes traveled up and down the length of my body before she put her chubby ass hand on her hip. "Who are you and what are you doing here?"

"Ask Tony."

"I don't need to ask Tony, muthafucka. I'm askin' you. Keep withholding answers, and we're gonna have ourselves a problem. Now, who are you?"

I didn't want to give her the satisfaction, but her homegirl looked terrified. It was my first day, and I didn't feel like starting off on the wrong foot. "Owen. I work for Tony."

A voice yelled out from a distance, but I wasn't able to hear a thing it said.

"Leave him alone y'all! Have a seat somewhere and calm down." She turned her attention to me and smiled. "Hey Owen, I'm Mariyah. I'm sorry about these two. It's been a hectic day, and it's only going to get worse from here. I hope you're ready for the ride."

"I am."

She also used her eyes to travel the length of my body. Her stare came off different. She was checking to see if I would be able to protect her daughter through thick and thin. No matter what came our way, she wanted reassurance that Ani would be in good hands.

"My loyalty will be earned. She's good with me." My answer satisfied her for now, but I was an outsider. My actions were going to have to prove my words to her.

"Alright everyone, have a seat. There are some things that we need to go over. Kin left something for you Ani, and it'll help you through your transition."

Tony pressed a few buttons, and a projector came from the ceiling. Everyone took a seat, and I stayed back by the door. It wasn't my place to blend in with the family. I was here for one reason and one reason only.

"Baby girl, if you're seeing this then that means I've been taken away. Before I get into everything, I would like to apologize for not being there for you all these years. I have my reasons, and if you are up for that conversation, then I'll be more than happy to have it with you. Unfortunately, baby, shit's about to get real and it's up to you to not fail under pressure. Don't worry. I'll be with you every step of the way. Mariyah and Tony know exactly what to do and how to train you up. You are a boss baby girl and never let anyone tell you otherwise. Hold your head up and know that you are about to run an empire. You will be feared, you will be love, and you'll be hated. Death will come knocking at your door more times than you can count. There are a few things that you'll need to do in order to prepare for your reign. Your apartment is no longer yours. The house that you are in was built for you. Ziggy will go over every security detail. Keep your head up, Ani'Yah. I love you past the moon and the stars. We'll catch up soon."

The man disappeared from the screen, and the tension in the room was thick. I don't know what I just got myself into, but there was no turning back. I'd made a commitment, and I was a man of my word. That's all I had to offer.

"Come on, Owen. They're going to need a minute to process the information that they just received. We gotta go get you fitted for your suit."

❧ 8 ❧

BRITTON MATTHEWS

Things were moving quickly for Ani. One minute she was a normal girl, and then the next she was the head of a damn drug empire. This was a soft spot for me, and I hated that I was finding myself back in this world.

Two years ago, I dated a man who was heavy in the streets of Philly. He had the game on lock, but the life that we were living was too much for me to handle. Fighting women left and right, dodging bullets, and catching bodies wasn't what I signed up for. A lot of bitches have it twisted when they say that they want to be gone off that *hood love*. They tend to forget what comes with that lifestyle.

DJ was my everything when I lived in Philly. He was my sun, my moon, and my stars. He was the air that I breathed, and he provided the supplements that I needed to make it through my days. Unfortunately, like all good love stories, ours came to an end when DJ wanted more than I was willing to give. I refused to take his last name or even bear his children for that matter. He wasn't giving up the game any time soon, and I refused to bring children into a fucked-up situation.

He couldn't deal with the fact that I was protecting us and our lively hood. Everyone knows that family is a weakness to anyone moving heavy weight. That's the easiest way to bring your enemies to their knees. One wouldn't think I knew much about the game, but I knew everything there was. DJ didn't shelter me from his life. I was there with him every step of the way. From re-ups to lavish meetings with the connect. If it involved the drugs, then baby I was there with his ass. You could call me his right hand woman. There wasn't a deal that went down without my knowledge.

If Ani was being sucked into this world, then I was going to be right there with her through it all. Ani was a soft soul and kind-hearted, but this wasn't the job for that. She was going to have to become feared and ruthless in a game full of men. They were like sharks. If they smelled fear, then they would bite into her and chew her up. Everything that Kindred worked for would go to waste.

Ziggy walked into the living room and looked at Ani. She was a space cadet at this point. She had zoned out, and it was evident on her face.

"Ani, are you ready for the briefing?"

Of course, she wasn't ready. Would *you* be ready for a briefing if you just found out that you were the head of a fuckin' cartel? Hell no you wouldn't, Ziggy! I wanted to scream out, but instead I hit him with a simple, "She'll be ready in five minutes." In return, he nodded and walked away.

"I'll be with you every step of the way. You're going to go in, listen to what they have to say, and then we go from there. Let's not put more stress on you than necessary, love. I got you. We are in this for life, mama." Her eyes glossed over, but she quickly wiped the tears away.

"Brit, I'm tired of feeling weak. The fact that I keep freaking out during everything is getting to me. I want to show the same type of confidence and authority that Kindred just showed. Even though he was on the other side of a video, he made me want to straighten up and get to it. These men are going to walk all over me right now, Brit. I don't want that."

"Well, what do you suggest we do about it?" I had a few ideas in mind. However, I wanted to see what she had to say.

Before she answered, she took a deep breath. "I guess I need to look the part. My current look isn't going to cut it."

Her outfit wasn't terrible, but it wasn't what a boss bitch should be wearing to her first meeting with her crew.

"Exactly, we'll have to deal with this for now while you're in the briefing, but once that's complete, we'll work on getting you a whole new wardrobe. We have our work cut out for us. Let me make a few calls, and we'll get the ball rolling."

Once she got her mind in order, we were able to get going. Apparently, we had to meet Kindred's people at a warehouse that wasn't too far from the safe house. I think I was more nervous than Ani that I had vowed never to be a part of this lifestyle again. I had vowed to run and never look back, but I had to be truthful with myself. All of this was making me miss DJ.

⚜

DARKNESS HAD FALLEN UPON US WHEN WE ARRIVED AT THE warehouse. We stepped out and were greeted by a big burly man with a form-fitting black suit. His skin was dark as midnight to the point that you could only see the whites of his eyes. Shit, looking at his big ass made me tap my purse to see if I had a Glock with me. He wasn't the type of nigga that you fight. A bullet to the head would do his ass just fine.

We approached, and when he opened his mouth, it was hard for me to contain my laughter.

"Hey y'all! Welcome! We've been waiting for your arrival."

This nigga was far too happy for me. How you look like a stone-cold killer on the outside but turn out to be a big bubbly piece of joy. It was not what I was expecting. Midnight, that's the name that I gave him, led us into the warehouse to a table full of people waiting on us.

They all stood when Ani walked in behind me.

"Welcome, Ms. Ani. We've been looking forward to this day. You've grown so much since the last time we saw you."

"I would like to first thank you all for coming, and I'd also like to apologize for not coming prepared. All of this was so sudden, and I don't know any of your names."

She handled that a lot better than I thought she would. She was seated at the table, and the meeting commenced.

Everyone that was seated at the table had been working for Kindred for years. From security to maids, to butlers, to airline pilots. He had it all. They informed Ani that they were at her service, and it was up to her if she wanted to keep them on retainer or not. She informed them that they would be able to keep their jobs, and they were grateful for that.

"Midnight" revealed himself to be Kindred's right hand. Something about him rubbed me the wrong way, and I was going to keep my eye on him. He was able to provide us with all the information that was needed in order for Ani to run things successfully. With the info given to her, she set up a meeting with all of her distributors. She wanted to know who they were, where they came from, and what territory they were holding down. I had to stop and smile because I couldn't believe how quickly she had turned around. Just this morning Ani was a scared, worrisome, twenty-four-year-old woman.

The meeting was done, and Ani had a few words with Nolton also known as Midnight. I continued to keep an eye on him even as my phone was ringing. He was giving me the creeps, and I refused to leave Ani alone with him for one second.

Without looking at the phone, I answered it. "Hello?"

"Damn, I missed that sexy ass voice." The phone fell out of my hand as my past came back to haunt me.

✴ 9 ✴

ANI MACK

I'd be a liar if I didn't say that I was overwhelmed. So much had happened in one day that it was going to take me a minute to grasp everything. I woke up a normal girl, living a normal ass life. Now, I must morph into this boss bitch, and I didn't know how to do that. My team is solid, so I know that they'll be there for me every step of the way.

Britton was hell-bent on helping me come into my role. She had me set aside my morning for shopping. My style reflected my life— simple and comfortable. Apparently, there's no room for comfortable and simplistic clothes in the drug game. A light knock on my door caused me from going down a deep dark hole. It had to be my mother because Brit wouldn't have knocked.

Against my better judgment, I let her come in. She smiled at me, but it didn't reach her eyes. If I had to guess, all of this was taking a toll on her too. My mother was never one to tell me how she was feeling, so I don't think that would change now. No matter what situation came our way, she would always say that she was fine. A regular person would admire her for that, but not me. I'm her daughter, and she should feel comfortable enough to let me know what's going on. I couldn't ignore the fact that her whole vibe was off. Hopefully, she'll tell me before her thoughts consume her and take her to a place of no return.

She began placing a few picture frames on the bare dresser. That sealed the deal that this was my new home. All of this was foreign territory, and it felt good to have a feeling of normalcy. Reaching the bed, she sat down on the bed and started fumbling with the comforter.

"Are you going to be okay, Ani?"

She was nervous, and Lord knows I was too. In all of my years on this earth, my mother never showed an ounce of fear. She would hold her head high and conquer whatever came her way. This was unfamiliar territory, and I needed to tread lightly.

"I'll be fine ma. You've raised me right. I'm gonna need you to be with me every step of the way. Do you think you can handle that? I don't want to bring you back into the life that you ran from."

Her hand moved up and halted my words. Her eyes met mine, and she just stared at me for a brief moment.

"I will be there for you, but there are some things that you have to experience and learn on your own. It's been twenty-two years, and I'm almost positive that the game has changed. I'll be learning all over again. However, I have faith in you, Ani."

She meant for her words to come off warm, yet they hit me like ice. In so many words, she was telling me that her past hurt wouldn't allow her to stand by my side during this transition. I understood her hurt, as well as her pain. It's my hope that one day she and my father would reach common ground and work out their issues.

"I understand." Her lips hit my cheek, and she left the room without any other words.

There wasn't any time to wallow around about her conversation. I needed to get ready before Britton came busting—

"Ani'Yah, why aren't you dressed? I told you to be ready at 9:30 a.m.! We are on a tight schedule. The first stop is getting that mane of yours taken care of. Then we're going to work on the clothes. Now get that ass out of bed!"

Before I could toss the cover off of me, she snatched it and flipped me out of bed onto the floor. If her loud ass mouth didn't wake me up, then that damn sure did it.

"I'll be back. I'm gonna get your coffee started. Get showered and dressed, Ani!" The door slammed behind her, and I went to handle my hygiene.

Stepping back into the room, I was met by the light-skinned man from yesterday. Seeing that I was only in my towel, a screech escaped my lips. "What the hell are you doing in here?" His head spun around, and he was just as surprised as me.

"My bad." He quickly closed his eyes and turned towards the door.

What is it with my damn security? Why do they always catch me when I'm half dressed?

"Ugh, just keep your eyes towards the door while I get dressed." He followed directions and clasped his arms behind his back. "What are you doing in here anyway?"

He started to turn around to answer, but I reminded him that I was getting dressed. Hopefully, he'd listen better when it came to my wellbeing.

"I was waiting on you to take you and the loud chick to your hair appointment. I knocked a few times and didn't get a response. I thought something was wrong, so I came in to see if you were good."

"This must be new to you too, huh?" He shrugged and chuckled. "Well, we have something in common. How about you let me finish getting dressed then we can get out of here?" I was dressed and ready in less than ten minutes. There wasn't a need for me to get cute. Britton was going to change all of that once my hair was done.

We arrived at the hair salon, and I was immediately thrown in a chair. My hair was flipped, clipped, and dipped. By the time she was finished, I didn't know who was staring back at me in the mirror. This was a grown ass woman in the mirror and not Ani.

"It's amazing how a simple haircut can go a long way." The stylist smiled at me and removed the cape. I tried to tip her for her services, but she refused. Apparently, it was already taken care of. "Anyone related to Kindred is a friend of mine."

"You knew my father?" I asked with my eyebrow raised.

It didn't matter if my mama and daddy weren't together. I wasn't about to let some chick try to get her claws in him. There was something in me, deep down, that hopes that maybe they could get it together.

"Oh no. I mean y-yes I did." Her eyes grew wide as she tried to think of something to say. "Yes, I've only known him for a few years. H-he helped out my mom a few times with her medicine. He's a really good man. You should be happy to have him as a father."

My eyes traveled the length of her body while my face was full of disgust mixed with uncertainty. For her sake, she better had been telling the truth. Walking away from her was probably for the best before I said something I had no business saying.

"Damn Ani, did you have to look at her like that?" Britton was standing there when everything happened but opted to be quiet. "Okay, I see that big bad bitch wants to come out and play. I'm loving this. She was right. A simple haircut will transform a woman."

I completely disregarded her words and started playing on my phone. "Where are we headed next?"

"Shopping!" She was so loud that it caused me to grimace. "We're going to turn you into the baddest bitch they've seen thus far."

❧ 10 ❧

KINDRED EDWARDS

Don't think for one second that this is what I wanted for my daughter. Most men in my position would love for their seeds to take over their throne while they sit comfortably in retirement, but this wasn't that. I wanted Ani to live a normal childhood and enjoy the fruits of my labor. She should be exploring the world, getting married, and making a family of her own. However, I knew in my heart that if she ever needed to step up and do what needed to be done, she would succeed.

"Sup, Tony. Tell me what's going on?" Tony was the only person that I allowed to visit me.

"Shit, Kin it's a lot going on. I'm still tryna find out who was following Ani and her friend while they were out grubbin'. Something tells me this ain't the Mexicans. They wouldn't do no stupid shit like that. If they wanted her dead, they wouldn't have chased her. This has to be personal, Kin. I'm trying to weed out the snake, but this shit ain't easy." The words came out of Tony's mouth effortlessly.

"What kind of training has Ani started? Does she know how to shoot? What's her running like? Does she have the stamina?" I fired off question after question. She had to be ready for this. Someone was coming for her, and they weren't going to stop until they killed her, or she killed them.

"About that..." Tony put his folded hands on the table and held his head down. Shit wasn't right, and he was going to tell me some bullshit.

"Tony, you better get to talkin' before they add murder to my charges."

"Man, it's only day two. She hasn't started any training yet. Her best friend thought it was best to help boost her confidence first. You know, take it easy during her first few days since this is a lot to process. They're out right now shopping and getting her hair done."

He sat back in his chair, and he was a lucky muthafucka. If he was any closer to me, then I was going to reach across this table and strangle the fuck outta him. Her life is in danger, and her ass thinks this shit is a fuckin' fashion show!

"Tony, what the fuck is going on out there. Come on, man. That shit is the last thing she needs to be worried about. The drug game ain't a fuckin' hair battle. Get my daughter into some fuckin' training classes right now." I spoke to him through gritted teeth so that the guards wouldn't hear me. "You know what? Set up a kidnapping right now. I know we have some niggas on our payroll. They need to assess her critical thinking skills. Do it NOW!"

"Aye Edwards! Cool down over there!" The guard tapped on his gun to let me know that he would shoot my black ass at the first chance he got.

"Here, I was able to pull a few strings, and they let me bring this in."

He slid a phone towards me across the table. I snatched it up and put it in my pants pocket before anyone could see. It's a bunch of hatin' ass niggas in here, and they all know who I am. They wouldn't hesitate to test me.

"Go handle that now." Tony nodded and left out of the visitation area.

As I was escorted back to my cell, I thought of a million different people that would be at my head. Shit, I had good standing relationships with the Mexicans and Italians so I could scratch them off the list. The Cubans and I didn't get along, but they stayed out of my way, and I stayed out of theirs. Thinking about this was causing my damn head to hurt. I needed to get through to Riyah, but that was going to be like pulling teeth.

11

ANI MACK

This day was going better than I expected. We'd torn down the mall and picked out some nice pieces for me. Britton was really helping me come into my own. Slowly but surely, I could feel myself coming into my own. I was on a high and nothing could knock me down.

The sun had disappeared by the time we were wrapping up at the last boutique. Owen was over in the corner taking a phone call and wasn't showing any signs of movement. My feet and lower back were killing me, and I didn't have time to wait around for him to finish his call. I motioned for him to pass me the keys, and he threw them my way. Brit and I began walking towards the car with the little bags that we had. Ziggy had come earlier to get most of the bags. We'd shopped so much that we wouldn't be able to fit it all in the truck with us.

"How are you feeling? Did this day help you at all?" Britton was so excited about all of this, and I couldn't even lie. This had boosted my confidence to the max. My hair was now short just above my shoulders while bouncing and flowing in the breeze.

"Yeah, I feel really good, and I owe it all to you. I would not feel this good if it wasn't for you," we placed the last of our little bags in the trunk and slammed it shut.

Before I could scream, a man in a black mask came up behind Britton and snatched her purse off her shoulder. She took off running after him, and I followed. The parking structure was about three stories high, and he chose to go up to the top instead of down and out.

Before I got too far, I remembered that I had the keys in my hand. I stopped running and went to the truck. I cranked it up and sped up the ramp. Two levels up I saw that Britton was tussling near another SUV just like this one. I drove right to them and prayed that I was able to stop the car in time without hitting them. My aim was to scare him into letting go of the purse and running.

Britton let the purse go and jumped out of the way. The car tapped the offender and sent him flying. He was laid out on the ground rolling over in pain.

"Brit, you okay? I need to call the police!"

"Bitch, have you lost your mind?" She came over and grabbed my phone slamming it on to the ground. "Girl fuck them police! You just almost killed a nigga! Let's put his ass in the trunk and then take him back to Tony. He should know what to do."

"Better yet, let's get our asses out of here and leave him right where he is. Someone will come and help him."

Before the words left my mouth, the doors to the black truck opened up, and two more men in ski masks jumped out and ran towards us. We took off running, but our skills were no match for theirs. They snatched both of us and placed a black cloth over our faces. I tried to fight them off as best as I could, but the chemical-drenched cloth was too much for me to handle.

⚜

A BRIGHT WHITE LIGHT CREPT THROUGH THE SLITS OF MY EYES AS I tried to remember what happened. It was all a blur, and the headache that I had was taking me through it. Trying to remember what happened was a struggle, but then I thought about Britton. My eyes popped open, and I started panicking. This seems to be a pattern for me. I had to get my shit under control.

"Aye Brit! Where are you?"

"Nice to have you join us, Ani'Yah."

The sound of my mother's voice filled the white room. My body froze, and I knew that I was in trouble. She only called me by my full name when I had fucked up. I didn't know what I did wrong this time. Shit, did I kill that man?

My vision returned, and I saw my mother sitting in a chair across from me with her arms folded and her legs crossed. Attitude etched her face, and my mind didn't understand why. Did she know what we just went through?

"Mama, before you go off. Please let me expl—"

She held her hand up to shut me up. Any other time in my life I would listen to my mother and respect her wishes, but I was fed up at this point. I've been chased, shot at, almost hit by a damn train, and kidnapped. It's only been two days since I came into this new role. This shit seemed never-ending, and they caught me off guard these last few times, but I promise to God that it won't happen again. Ignoring her, I continued talking.

"I need to find out who did this. My life has been played with far too many times for my liking, and I'm not going to keep dealing with this shit. I'm not trained for these kinds of situations. However, today was going to be the last day for this.

"Mom, I appreciate what you're about to tell me, but I'm not interested in knowing anything further. Right now, I need to find someone who will train me to be able to handle high-intensity situations like this."

I stood up from the chair and stumbled, but I walked out and realized that we were back in the house. I still didn't know where Britton was, so I stood outside the door and called her name.

"If you didn't just try to get gangsta with me you would know that she's good and she's upstairs resting. Go take a nap and then we can work on finding you a trainer. I have a feeling that the shit that happened today was a *push* from a certain someone. I'll find out, but I'm almost certain that I'm right."

My mom walked off and went to find answers for today. I, on the other hand, went to my room and fell into the bed. Sleep came and took over all of my thoughts.

12

MARIYAH MACK

Kindred had single-handedly fucked up my night. When Tony brought in a sleeping Ani and Britton, I knew that this was his doing. He used to do things like this all the time with me to "prepare" me in case anything happened to me. I understood why he was doing it, but there were so many other ways to go about this. Why did he have to catch her off guard? It's fine for right this second, but in a minute I'm about to find out all the answers that I need.

I went in search of the dumb ass who was supposed to protect these girls. Tony was set up in the guest house, so that's where I started. I found Tony in his room sleeping with not a care in the world.

"Wake yo ass up, Tony!" He jumped out the bed disoriented and went to reach for his gun.

"If you touch it, I'm going to shoot you in the foot, Tony. And I don't wanna shoot you." I clicked a bullet in the chamber so quick that his eyes almost popped out of his head.

"Riyah, what the hell is going on? Why the fuck do you have a gun pointed at me." He was wiping sleep out of his wide eyes.

"Did Kindred put you up to the shit with Ani?"

"Riyah, put that damn gun down, and yeah, he was up to it." I placed the gun by my side and waited for him to keep talking. "He wasn't interested in the fact that Ani has yet to do any real work dealing with the business. He lost his mind when he found out that she was shopping and shit. And before you open your mouth, I tried to explain to him that her friend was just trying to help boost her confidence. You know how he is, Riyah. He wasn't going to accept that. We gotta toughen her up. Someone's after her, and I hate to say it, but it's an inside job. We're gonna have to be on our toes and weed them out."

Just knowing that Ani had her first real enemy

was enough to make my heart race. This was serious, and he was absolutely right. She wasn't trained for this. Tomorrow she was going to be in for a rude awakening.

⚜

THE BUCKET FULL OF COLD WATER WAS READY TO SLAP ANI AND Britton in the face. Somehow Britton ended up in Ani's bed, even though we had set her up in a bedroom of her own. The two of them have been inseparable since Britton got here. If Ani was going to go through training, Britton would have to go through it as well. She was her right hand and needed to be prepared for anything. I wasn't too worried about Britton because she's shown that this world wasn't unfamiliar territory to her. It wasn't my place to ask about her past because sooner or later it would reveal itself.

Cold water splashed in their faces and hell broke loose. There were a few obscenities, and their eyes grew wide when they saw that it was me.

"Let's go, throw on these clothes. Your training starts now."

13

OWEN PIERCE

When Tony told me about the kidnapping plan, I thought it was some of the stupidest shit I'd ever heard. There were a few other avenues they could have gone down before they got to that one. Yeah, lil mama needed training, but damn, abducting her ain't the way to go about it. However, it wasn't my place to say anything. She'll learn how to deal with this on her own. If I were her, I wouldn't be taking orders from anyone. Her pops wasn't holdin' much rank behind those steel bars.

Once we made it back to the estate, Tony told me to head home for the night. He knew shit was gonna go south with the eldest Ms. Mack and didn't want me to have any parts of that. It was still my first day. She was a firecracker, and I would stay clear of her until a conversation was needed.

I headed out the gates to kick back at Camille's house even though everything inside of me was telling me to take Ms. Mack up on her offer to stay in the guest house. In theory, it would have worked, but I couldn't do that to Camille. We were like oil and water most days, and other days we clicked. We were still trying to figure the shit out.

The moment my key entered the lock, the door flew open and on the other side stood Camille with a tear-stained face. How long had her crazy ass been standing right there and why was she standing there crying? I couldn't deal with any more drama today. I just wanted to lay down and get some sleep. Was that too much to ask? I gently moved her to the side and walked in the door while loosening my tie.

"This is what we're doing now? You're going to just walk past me like everything is fine? Owen, you've been gone all day, and I haven't heard from you once. I don't like worrying about you." She hugged herself as more tears fell down her face.

"Don't."

You would have thought I told her to go to hell and never come back the way that her mood changed.

"Who is she? I know you've been with another woman all day. I followed you! Tell me who the fuck she is!" She charged towards me and tried to fight me.

A chuckle came out of my mouth as I held onto her wrists.

"You're bat shit crazy for real, ma. What the fuck did I tell you I was doing when I left this fuckin' house this morning? Didn't I tell you that I was starting a new gig? Use this thick ass head of yours to think of the many things I could have been doing. Lemme give you a hint. It wasn't cheating!"

Her eyes grew wide as my anger started to get the best of me. I tend to keep shit simple with people because I know how bad my temper is and I've worked hard to cage that beast. Camille was poking at him, and if she kept this crazy ass shit up, then she was going to wake him the fuck up.

Releasing her arms, I walked off to the bedroom. She was hot on my heels, but she refrained from opening her mouth. It's been a long ass day, and all I wanted to do was eat, shower, and sleep. Tony let me know before I left that shit was going to get intense for me. I had to complete a special type of training, but I wasn't too worried about that.

"Baby—"

I turned around to face her, and our noses almost touched. I took a step back from her, and she dropped down to her knees. Whenever she didn't get her way, she would try to use sex as a bargaining tool. I tried to not look down at her while she undid my zipper. If I looked at her, then I wouldn't be able to control my actions. Something about her dark brown eyes and full pouty lips always made me give in.

Against my better judgment, we locked eyes as soon as she freed me from my dress pants. She coated her lips in saliva and placed the tip in her mouth. I tried to protest, but the feeling of those soft warms lips had me stuck. Her ass was sucking like her rent money depended on it.

Her mouth was golden, and not too long after, I was pulling her head away releasing her death grip on me. She stood up wiping her mouth and crawled on the bed with her ass in the air. I couldn't resist the feeling brewing inside of me even if I wanted to. My second head was thinking for me. Opening the drawer, I grabbed a condom and tore the foil. As fate would have it, Camille turned around with anger on her face.

"What the hell do you need that for?" Her tone started harsh, but then she switched to pouting.

This shit was never-ending, and I didn't have time to go back and forth with her. It was just too much. It was a never-ending saga with her. She knew that I wasn't ready for kids and I don't think I'll be ready any time soon. How was I going to bring a shorty into this world when I'm not even financially stable? That's a problem that a lot of people have, and I refuse to go down that path. I've seen it happen with far too many people.

"Shut up and turn your ass around."

I yanked her ass to me while putting the condom on. Her words weren't what I wanted to hear right now. The sound of moaning was the only thing on my mind. Her ass was in the air, but the arch in her back needed improvement. I placed my forearm in her back and pushed it down. With my free hand, I spread one of her cheeks and slammed my width into her. A high-pitched screech escaped from her mouth, and that was all I wanted to hear from her today. As I rammed in and out of her wetness, she clawed at my arms.

"Ugh, I just can't get enough of this, Owen! I love you so much. We're meant to be."

We'd never established love in this situation, and I wasn't trying to start today. I wrapped my hand around her throat and gave it a light squeeze. With my other hand, I gripped her waist because I was nearing my peak. I slammed into her one more time before I pulled out and stroke everything out into the condom. With her begging for a family, I couldn't take any chances. She was going to be pissed, but it is what it is. We weren't ready for that. I walked into the bathroom to flush the condom.

When I finished, I took a shower and walked out of the bathroom to Camille sitting in the middle of the bed cradling a glass of wine. Tears fell from her eyes and shit was about to hit the fan.

"What are we doing, Owen? Do you not love me?" My head fell towards my chest, and it sent her through the roof. "We can make this work, Owen. I can be everything you need. I promise that I'll get my emotions under control."

She threw back the liquor, placed the glass on the side table, and crawled over to me.

"We good, shorty. Stop this dramatic ass shit."

"Owen, what's it going to take for you to engage in a conversation with me? Why are you so short with me?"

"Camille, if you want to have a conversation with me then give me something to talk about. This one right here isn't what I'm interested in. I'm going to tell you this one more time. I'm not ready to have kids or anything associated with that. I'm trying to work on gettin' this money. The quicker you realize that the better off we'll be."

That answer seemed to satisfy her, but that would only work for so long. We'd be talking about this sooner rather than later. She laid her head on my chest, and we both dozed off.

"What's good, old man?"

I was driving back to Ani's estate for work this morning and decided to give my pops a call. We didn't talk as much as I wanted to even though we still had a tight relationship.

He let out a low chuckle that turned into a coughing fit. "I got your old, Owen. Don't forget who taught you everything you know."

"You good over there? Where'd that cough come from?"

"Boy, don't worry about me. I just have a little tickle in my throat that's all. Focus on that your new job and your woman. I'm gonna be good." My father never wanted me to worry about him, and if something were going on with him, I would have to figure it out myself.

"Tell me how the jobs are going? How's Camille?" He started coughing again. This time I ignored it like he told me to.

"The job is decent. I can't go into detail about what I do, but it's paying well. Camille is Camille. Same shit, different day."

"You know I don't like that little girl no ways. Why you still with her?"

Honestly, I didn't know why I was still with her. We've only been together for about eight months. Every day was a different battle for us, and it was starting to wear me thin. Something drew me towards her in the beginning, but she was showing her true colors lately. That bipolar shit wasn't what I was interested in. She needed to get a handle on it and soon.

"We click, pops. That's all I can say."

"Hell, you can so call "click" with her, but that doesn't mean she's the one you should be spending the rest of your life with. I don't like the vibes she gives off, son. Something ain't right with her, but who am I to say anything. If she's the one, Lord help me, I have no choice to accept it. If she's not the one and the right one comes along, I'll accept her too, but you gotta figure that out for yourself." Pops loved spittin' gems early in the morning, and I couldn't help but listen.

"Nah, I don't think she's the one. She satisfies the crave for now though."

"I didn't need to know all of that, but I understand. I need you to find a good woman to settle down with. You know I'm not going to live forever."

"Man, you're the healthiest man that I know. You're probably going to live longer than me. And as far as a woman, eh, it's complicated."

"Complicated huh? Tell me why."

"I only say complicated because we can't be together."

"Yeah that sounds complicated to me, but you still aren't telling me why it's complicated."

He was pushing for more out of me than I was willing to give. One thing I didn't do was keep information from my pops.

"Be-because she's my boss." A deep sigh came out of my mouth as silence came from the other the end of the phone. "Hello? Pops, you still there?"

"Yeah son, I'm here." He took a deep breath then let it out causing the coughing to start back up.

"Pops," I called out.

"Owen, I'm fine. I'm gonna say this before I let you get back to work. If she's worth it, then fight for it. She's got you stuttering like a little school boy. I like her already. When the time comes, make sure you bring her by to meet me."

"Yeah, I'm not sure that's gonna happen. But hey, I just got to work, so I'm gonna call you a little later to check on you. Take care of yourself."

"I see you ignored my words and that's fine. One of these days you're gonna wish you had listened to me. But gone get to work, tell Tony I said thanks again for bringing you into that job. I'll talk to you later." That coughing started again and then the phone disconnected.

I made a mental note to check on him as soon as I could. He was hiding something from me, and we were better than that. I couldn't dwell on it too much because when I pulled into the estate, Ms. Mack had Ani running up and down the driveway. This was going to be a long day. I needed to focus on my job and staring at her in little ass shorts wasn't going to help with shit.

14

BRITTON MATTHEWS

THREE WEEKS LATER

Now my mama ain't raise me to disrespect my elders, but Mama Mack was being a little extra. Who knew that this little short ass woman was so damn aggressive. She had one more time to yell at me before I started yelling back. She had lost her mind with some of the shit she had us doing. I'm a personal trainer, and she had me out here believing that I was out of shape.

Every day for the past three weeks we were engaged in around the clock training. I don't know much about being the head of a cartel, but I'm pretty fuckin' sure that El Chapo didn't do this shit! Why the hell did we have to? My body hurt in places that I didn't know could hurt. Shit, it even hurt to blink. The only upside about all of this was seeing Ani's transformation. She was a beast during this training. The first few days were full of complaints, but that's to be expected. She had never engaged in such intense training.

Mama Mack had us doing everything from running long distances, shooting, shooting while running, and a whole bunch of other shit. It was difficult, but we pushed each other and got through it. Thankfully, Ms. Mack was nice enough to give us the afternoon off, and I was going to partake in sleeping. That was the only thing I was concerned about.

My eyes had only been closed for about twenty minutes before the buzzing of my phone woke me up. I knew exactly who it was, and I wished that he would stop calling. We didn't have anything to talk about at this point. He made his decision a long time ago, and I made mine.

"What do you want DJ?" My words came out groggily.

"Is that the way you talk to your future husband?"

Shit, those words right there woke my ass up. We were not about to start this shit, especially not on my day off.

"Boy, who the fuck you talkin' to? My future husband is somewhere in Wakanda training with T'Challa and Okoye. It doesn't sound like you're there, so we can't be talkin' about you!"

"Aye Brit, stop fuckin' playin' me to the left. Just because we're separated right now doesn't mean that we're done. I told you once before, and I'll tell you again. We are in this for life. Got it?"

"Nigga—"

"What the fuck did I just say?"

The only person that could take my wild mouth and outlandish persona was DJ. He was my kryptonite, and there was no denying the way that he made me feel. Just hearing him say my name and using his deep voice caused me to reminisce on the good times that we shared. However, those memories faded when I started thinking about what caused us to separate. Even though we were the same, we were still different. He wanted to have his cake and eat it too.

"Goodbye, DJ. I hope you have a great day." I hung up the phone, and he called back five times before I answered again.

"What—"

"Aye, where you at so that I can fix that foul ass mouth? It's obvious that you missed daddy, and that's why you're acting out," he said, a bit too calm for me.

His voice was always one to make me feel a certain way. It was heavy in bass and shook my body to the core every time he whispered in my ear. Just hearing him talk to me like this had me biting my lip and closing my eyes.

"Stop fighting destiny, Britton. We're meant to be."

I always thought that he was the one for me. However, our views were so different. We didn't want the same things in life, and I didn't want to compromise for a man. Why should I do that when he wasn't willing to do the same for me?

Against my better judgment, I gave in.

"I'm at Ani's house right now DJ. I'll call you tonight when I finish with some things to see if we can meet up. For now, I'm about to take a nap, and that doesn't include me staying on the phone with you like we're teenagers."

He let out a chuckle, and we said our goodbyes.

I guess it wasn't meant for me to get sleep this afternoon. As soon as I hung up with DJ, Ani came busting in my room and flopped her thick ass on the bed. This training was stackin' her body up nicely. She laid next to me and heavily sighed. I ignored her attempts to get my attention, but that only lasted so long. Her ass climbed in my face and started pulling my hair.

"Ani, I love you, and you know this, but I won't hesitate to flip you on to this hard ass floor if you don't stop pulling my damn hair." I flipped her off me, and she fell on the bed laughing.

"Brit, I need to get ready for this meeting. Can you help me find something to wear? Also, I need to figure out what I'm going to do with this hair of mine."

Now she was talking my language. As much as I wanted to nap, I knew she was going to need my help.

❧ 15 ❧

ANI MACK

The car ride to the warehouse was calm and cool. It was now or never, and I needed to meet the people that work under me. It's been long enough since my father's been locked up and they needed to know what direction we were moving in. Brit placed a comforting hand on my bouncing knee to settle me down. She mouthed to me "everything is going to be fine", and I appreciated that. This shit wasn't going to be easy by far, but if it were easy, then everyone would be doing it.

For the past few weeks along with my physical training, I've been catching up on everyone that works for us. From their territory to their families and down to their secret baby mamas, I needed to know their strengths and weaknesses. If it had the potential to fuck up our money, then I needed to know about it. Most of them were clean, but some of them had some explaining to do.

Before I dug my nails into them too deep, I needed to see how they were going to accept me. They hadn't been under a woman's leadership, and that might take some getting used to. This is a male-dominated field, but they were going to have to learn that Ani Mack was going to be the best that ever did it.

The car came to a stop, and my nerves had finally settled. I was ready to get this shit moving. Owen came to open the car and looked at me. His eyes were telling me a story, and I didn't know what to think of it. He sized me up and nodded his head. I guess that was his way of saying that he approved. Not sure why he felt the need to do that, I didn't need his approval. However, my confidence was telling me otherwise. Britton had picked out a killer suit for me, and it had my ass on a high. I'm not one to get excited about clothes or anything. However, Britton really did her thing.

At this moment, no one walking this earth could hold a candle to me. The navy-blue suit was tailored to perfection. The jacket was snug against my upper body, while the slacks hugged on my tiny waist and plump ass like a glove. They stopped right above my ankles, forcing your attention to the sky-high Louboutin's with an ankle strap. She paired it with a flowing white blouse that showed off a just enough cleavage to get you thinking. Hopefully, I didn't look like a steak in front of these wild dogs. I couldn't help what my mama gave me.

"You gonna be okay?" I nodded at him, and he led us into the warehouse.

In the middle of the floor was a table that was occupied by all of my father's lieutenants except for one. The sound of our heels clicking against the concrete floor stopped the chatter, and all the attention was on Britton and me.

"We lettin' women into the warehouse now? Aw shit, did Big Kin finally listen to me and get entertainment for our meetings?"

A man by the name of Marlon laughed along with a few others. He pulled a band of money from his pocket and slapped it on the table.

"Lil mama you can start with me first."

A deep sigh escaped out of my mouth as I walked to the head of the table. Britton stood behind me, and Owen was posted at the door.

"First and foremost, my name ain't lil mama. It's Ani, and you will address me as such. Secondly, I don't know who you think I am, but I'm not one to play with."

He stood up from the table like he was really about that life. Owen walked towards me while reaching for his gun, and I had to stop him.

"Aye bitch, I don't know who the fuck you think you talkin' to, but it ain't me. Watch yo fuckin' mouth when it comes to me. Can somebody please tell me who the fuck is this and why is she even here?"

Looks of confusion flashed across everyone faces except for one. A man, with thick dreads, at the end of the table was leaned back in his chair with a smirk on his face. He smiled showing a mouth full of gold teeth, and then he winked. Our eyes connected and fire danced from the top of my body down to the white polish on my toes.

"Aye mane, calm all that down. Let her talk," his words came out with a deep accent.

If my memory served me correct, his name was Emmanuel, and he ran things up and down the southern states. He was of Haitian descent and lived that "zoe pound" life. He's the type of guy that my mama told me to stay away from.

"Man, fuck her. She ain't 'bout to come in here tellin' me what the fuck to do." He slammed his fists down on the table.

I pulled my strap from my back and pointed towards him. Two clean shots had him falling to the floor clawing away at the burning sensation in his chest. I thought I would feel sad when I caught my first body, but I didn't. It was as if a shock wave of ecstasy ran through me. Disrespect will not be tolerated, and if I didn't make an example out of him now, then everyone would try me.

"Britton, can you hand me the iPad please?" Brit handed me the iPad, and I flipped to his profile.

"Handle the funeral arrangements and make sure that we send flowers. Also, set up his wife and children. They shouldn't suffer because his parents didn't raise him to respect women in positions of power." A few men walked into the warehouse, and I knew that was the clean-up crew from their profiles.

"Hey Ms. Ani, I'm Timbs, and I work for Lady Landry Cleaning. I'll be handling your *situations* from here on out," he spoke in a thick New York accent, and it confirmed why they called him Timbs.

They removed Marlon from the warehouse, and I continued with my meeting.

"I don't like to start off meeting people this way. However, I was left with no choice. If you respect me, I'll respect you. And before you say it, I know that respect is earned and not given. We will earn each other's respect during this transition. Deal?"

I looked around the room and stared at each of them in the eyes except for Emmanuel. I wouldn't get through this meeting if I looked at him.

"Like I was saying I'm Ani. Ani Mack, I am the daughter of Kindred Edwards. I will be taking over his duties while he completes his bid."

Chatter erupted around the room just as I had expected.

"I know you are all wondering what happened and why you weren't informed about his incarceration, but it was on a need to know basis. He's only been there for a little while and that's all I can say. The less you know, the better you'll be if you're ever questioned by anyone.

"Now with that being said, nothing has changed. Most things will remain the same. We may switch up a few things like delivery schedules and such, but I'll be directly contacting the people that are affected by this change."

The door behind us opened and in walked the late comer.

"Sorry for being late, my plane had trouble comin' in from Philly."

Britton gasped, and I hung my head. I had been holding on to this secret for a while and hated that everything was coming to the light. I knew that this was going to shake Britton to the core, and I hated that I couldn't tell her. It wasn't my place to tell her everything that she needed to know about DJ. That was something that he had to do.

DJ was one of the first people that I read about when I started reviewing everyone's files. Apparently, he's been under my father's wing since he was sixteen and one of his best sellers. He had the whole east coast on lock. I've been through his file twice to see if there was anything dirty about him, but he was the cleanest ones that I'd come across. He dabbled with a few women here and there, but that wasn't anything new to me. Britton already knew about that. From what I can see, he's on the up and up now. He took his seat, and I continued with the meeting.

Things went unusually well after the Marlon situation. No one else tested me. We ended the meeting on a good note, and everyone started to go their separate ways. Most of them had planes to catch.

They had work to be done and didn't need to be gone for too long. However, two people stayed behind.

"Beautiful gal you are." Emmanuel walked over to me and sat on the table in front of me. He flashed that mouth full of gold, and I found myself melting again.

I nervously looked around the room to see if anyone had seen my reaction. Low and behold, Owen was tucked off in the corner with his arms folded. A scowl covered his face, and for the life of me, I couldn't understand why.

"Manny, don't you have a plane to catch?"

My mouth was dry, and my hands were moist with sweat. He placed a finger at the top of my arm and moved it slowly down until he reached my wrist. Against the suggestion of my soaking and throbbing honey pot, I removed his hand from mine.

"Manny... your plane?"

"The pilot waits for me. I don't rush fo' dem."

"I understand what you're saying, but there's work to be done. You have yourself a good night."

I grabbed the iPad off the table and went for my phone, but Manny snatched it. He held it up to my face to unlock it. Before I could process what was taking place and then protest it, he was calling himself and locking his number in.

"That's an invasion of privacy," I sassed with my hands on my hips.

"I'll sho' ya an invasion gal. Alright?" Grabbing my hand, he placed a kiss on it and walked out the door.

"Ani, can we please leave?" Britton stomped up to me with an attitude and her arms folded. Her body language told one story, while her face told another.

"She's good, Ani."

DJ walked up to Britton and wrapped his arms around her. Again, her face and her body weren't on the same page. Her body damn near melted in his arms, but her eyes rolled.

"Ani, if you leave me here with this man, I'm going to have to rethink our friendship."

Britton could rethink our friendship all she wanted. She loves that man, and it's obvious that he loves her. They needed to figure out what they were going to do, and it was best if I stayed out of it.

"DJ, take care of her, or you know how I'm comin'."

"You got it, *Boss Lady.*" Him saying Boss Lady had a nice ring to it.

There was still so much for me to learn. However, that put a smile on my face. I started walking out the door just as Britton cried for me to come back. Her cries were falling on deaf ears because I wasn't going to save her. She was on her own.

❧ 16 ❧

BRITTON MATTHEWS

Ani and DJ had me fucked up. This wasn't how this night was supposed to go. Why didn't she let me know beforehand that he was one of the workers? His ass came strolling in the meeting late as if he owned the fuckin' place. And let's not overlook the fact that he looked as good as the first time we met. This was far too much all at once.

"Come on. You might as well let me buy you dinner."

My stomach was growling, and I wasn't going to pass up a free meal. I may be a personal trainer, but I still like to eat. With his hand outstretched, DJ flashed a smile and waited for me to take his hand.

"I can manage. Thank you." With a little extra switch in my step, I walked out the door into the night.

The moon was full, and the weather was perfect. This city had a way of being breathtaking even after the sun has gone down. The breeze ripped through my shirt and caused a shiver to run through me. I wasn't as dressed up as Ani, but I was still professional in a black pencil skirt, a white dress shirt, and a pair of tan strappy heels. It was simple, but it worked on my thick ass body.

"You wouldn't be shiverin' if you had on proper clothes." DJ walked up to me and placed his suit jacket around me. "When you start walkin' out the house in tight ass shit showin' off your body?"

"Since I got grown and single. I gotta find a man out here in these Chicago streets. You know what I'm sayin'?" This shit was funny to me, but apparently it wasn't as amusing to him. He grabbed me by the hand and yanked me into an embrace.

"I don't care what niggas you were messin' around with during my absence. Dead that shit. I'm home Bri, remember that."

He hasn't called me Bri in a very long time. Just hearing my name roll off his tongue had me stuck. My eyes fell into his intense gaze, and I was spent. His cologne had intoxicated me, and I was ready to risk it all for DJ. Old feelings that I had suppressed a long time ago were resurfacing, and I didn't know which way to go. Our eyes searched for the unknown as questions of "what if" and "where do we go from here" ran through our veins.

At the same time, I could feel my body submitting to him. My lips quivered as they gravitated towards his. The pulsating sensation between my thighs was deadly. His hold on my waist grew tighter, and we engaged in a passionate kiss. In this moment, everything between us felt right. This kiss sealed the deal on him being the one for me. We had a lot to work through, and things weren't going to be easy.

"Get a room!" Ani called out as her car pulled off.

I flipped her off and continued looking at DJ. That's when flashes of the men currently occupying my attention came to the forefront of my mind. I was going to need to cut ties with all of them before DJ killed them. His temper wasn't anything to play with, especially when it comes to me.

"Dead it all before I get to 'em," he said while holding my face in his hands.

"I don't know what you're talkin' about."

I stepped out of his embrace and continued walking to his car. He didn't say a word while he opened the door. However, I could feel the hole that he was staring in the back of my head. He was dying to figure out who had the pleasure of occupying Ms. Britton's time. In all honesty, in the two years that I've been here, only two men have had the privilege of occupying my time. DJ was always in the back of my mind so things couldn't flourish even if they wanted to. My heart was with him whether I liked it or not.

A little while later we were arriving at a nice restaurant along the river. We were immediately seated, and wine was poured into my glass. I had half a mind to take it to the head, but the lady in me wouldn't allow it. Dinner was served, and the conversation was light. We were both lost in our thoughts that we didn't know what was going to come of this. It's like we knew that we were meant to be together, yet, there was an elephant in the room. We didn't want the same things out of this life. I wanted marriage and kids without the dope game.

There wasn't room in my life for me to be married to someone that was in as heavy as he was. I refuse to be the one to wake up in the middle of the night to a phone call saying that they found his body parts floating down the Chicago River. I refused to be the one to have to explain to my kids why they have to talk to their father behind a glass. My heart won't allow it.

"Listen, I know you're worried about a few things, and I want to clear that shit up. What's the difference between me workin' in this business and you workin' in this business? You're Ani's right hand, second in command, so you're no different than me now. You're connected to her, so now you're a target just like me."

It was obvious that he meant no harm with his words. However, they hit me deep and hard. He was right about it all. I hated to admit to it, but there was no escaping it.

"Exactly, now tell me why we can't pick up where we left off, and I make you my wife."

"Playboy, it's not that easy, and if it was, then I don't want no parts of it. Yes, you're right, and it doesn't taste good saying that, but we can't start over where we left off. Philly wasn't peaches and cream. We can't just *pick up where we left off*. We have a LOT of making up to do. If we're gonna do this, then you need to *date* me. Got it?"

"Fuck you mean I gotta date you? What kinda stupid shit is that, Bri? I know everything there is to know about you."

He continued his rant while I sat back in my seat with my arms folded. He could do all of this talking until he's blue in the face, but I was standing firm in what I said. Letting him pick up where he left off would be too easy for DJ.

"Earn me," I said while standing up from the chair. I pulled a few bills out of my purse and placed them on the table. The area was pretty busy at this time, so I was able to disappear into the crowds of people before DJ could catch me.

❧ 17 ❧

KINDRED EDWARDS

"She caught her first body? How did that happen?"

Tony had come to my visitation to keep me up to date with everything that was going on. Even though I was behind bars, it was still business as usual. Hearing that Ani caught a body a few weeks ago had me heated, but knowing that she offed one of the lieus was what sent me through the roof.

"You don't wanna even know the other shit's she's done. Don't get me wrong. Baby girl is doing the damn thing. Profits up damn near twenty percent and it's only been a few weeks, but nigga, we've created a monster."

"Who the hell is we? I ain't have no parts in that?" The words left my mouth as I remembered that I had Ani kidnapped. Did that set off the change in attitude? I didn't think it would cause her to be droppin' bodies like flies.

"*We* have created a monster."

Mariyah walked in the room with a scowl on her face. I hadn't seen her up close in twenty-two years. She hadn't aged and honestly looked better than the last time I saw her. She wore a long-sleeved sweater that showed off some cleavage with a pair of skin-tight blue jeans. She knew what she was doing when she wore that, especially when she placed stiletto pumps on her feet. She looked damn good.

Never in a million years did I think that Mariyah would visit me while I was in here, especially not after one of our many heated discussions. She yelled at me and said that she wouldn't come visit my black ass if I got locked up for more than twenty-four hours.

"What do you mean that you've created a monster?"

"She's not necessarily a monster, but she's exceeded our expectations, Kindred. She's far better at this than we thought she would be. We all figured that this would take some getting used to. Yet she picked up everything quickly, and has even started pushing better ideas."

Just hearing them talk about the woman that Ani had become caused a smile to form on my face. To know that my own flesh and blood was taking this company to another level was more than I could have ever asked for.

"Are you any closer to finding out who's after her?" They both shook their heads, and it infuriated me. "Nolton is scheduled to be here after y'all. I'm gonna see if the streets have been talkin'."

As we continued talkin', I found myself constantly sneaking looks at Mariyah. Little did she know, she still had my heart in her hands. I loved every day since the first day I laid eyes on her. I hate that we weren't able to work this shit out, and I take full responsibility for it.

Tony caught on to what I was doing and smirked. He was probably the only person that knew exactly how I felt about her. Over the years, Tony would give her money for her and Ani and say it was from him. However, it really came from me. I knew that she wouldn't accept it if it had come directly from me. He agreed to do that for me, and I appreciate it.

We continued to talk until their time was up. Saying goodbye to her was the hardest part. I didn't want the time to come to an end. Seeing her face gave me a little bit of comfort. Knowing that she came to see me even after promising never to step foot in this place gave me hope for the future.

Once they left, the guard informed me that my next visitor was here. Nolton came strolling into the room with a mean mug on his face, and his vibe was off. I've been around this nigga long enough to know when shit was bothering him. He was like a brother to me, and I helped raise him when his parents were killed. He didn't know that they were killed at the hands of my brother Kendrell, and I planned on keeping that secret even in death.

"What's on ya mental, Nole? You comin' in here fire hot. Tell me what's good?"

"Shit, you tell me what's good, Kindred. You get locked up and the daughter that you didn't even raise—"

"Watch ya self when you're speakin' on her. Tread lightly, or I'll forget you're my best friend," I warned him. His eyes turned into thin slits, and I knew that we would never be the same.

"How are you going to leave *everything* to someone that doesn't know shit about this game? I've been there with you from the beginning, from our days as corner boys to the day that the FEDS came and locked your black ass up. This was supposed to be mine, Kindred. MINE!" he roared and pounded his fists on the table. The guard started walking towards us, and I held up my hand assuring him that everything was good. Once word got around that I was in here the guards started shaping up. They knew that my name held weight in these streets and not to fuck with me.

"First and foremost, I never promised you a damn thing, Nolton. You knew damn well that the next person in line was my seed. And let's not act like you aren't enjoying the fruits of her labor, my nigga. You're eatin' good over there, so my question is, what's really the problem?"

He sat back in his seat and folded his arms across his fat ass stomach.

"I don't want no woman tellin' me what to do. Her and her little ass friend walkin' round this bitch barkin' orders and shit in six-inch heels and tight ass suits. Nah, I ain't cut out for that shit."

"You ain't cut out for that shit? Nigga, you ain't cut out for a lot of shit, but yet you still in it. If you can't handle taking orders from women, then nigga your mental is more fucked up than I thought. You might wanna see a therapist about that. Now either you get with the program, or you can get the fuck on. Plain and simple. You need to decide before you walk yo big ass out of this visitation room."

Fire was burning within me. I wanted to fuck this nigga up. Kendrell told me too many times to count to watch out for his ass. He's greedy and selfish, and those two things don't work well together in this business. His words were coming true before my eyes, and I hated that I didn't dead his ass a long time ago.

"You take it easy, Big Kin. I heard that someone's been after baby girl. I pray that they don't get their hands on her. Anyway, I'll be seeing you soon." He winked at me while standing up from his chair.

I reached for his neck, but they had my cuffs chained to the floor. He quickly ran out of the visitation room without any other words. Something was telling me that he was the one after Ani, but I didn't want to present this information to anyone without certain facts. I needed to really get my ears to the streets and get to the bottom of this before someone ended up dead.

✣ 18 ✣

ANI MACK

The past few weeks have been a roller coaster. My life has been threatened on multiple occasion. However, it comes with the territory. Someone was after me, and I wasn't going to stop until I found them. Business, on the other hand, was booming and profits were even up. However, for tonight, I was putting all of that to the side. I was going to enjoy life as a "normal" girl.

Ever since that little encounter with Manny at the first meeting, we've been conversing off and on. Nothing too heavy but just enough to make a girl feel wanted. He was smooth and charming. Yet, I wasn't sure if I was ready to take things to another level with him. Tonight would be the deciding factor. He had flown in from Miami for this date, and my anxiety was starting to get the best of me. Thankfully, I had Britton here to help me.

"Damn, you killin' it out here in this! That body looks tight as hell, Ani," Britton hyped me up as I twirled in the mirror for her.

Today I donned a sexy white body con dress with a black biker jacket and strappy heels around my ankles. Even though Manny and I had been conversing, I never gave in to his many attempts to take me out. When I finally caved in and told everyone, they ended up telling me how much they were against it. They thought that he had ulterior motives. I, on the other hand, saw a different side of him. He was a man that was feared by many, but they didn't know the real *him*. He's funny, cute, and charming.

"You better call me if anything happens. DJ and I will come to your rescue with guns blazing."

I knew that she was absolutely serious, and I couldn't help but laugh. My best friend was a rider, and I wouldn't be as successful as I am without her.

"Thank you, but that's not necessary. Even though he's coming to pick me up, Owen won't be too far behind. He refuses to leave me alone with him. He claims that he has an ulterior motive. I don't get that vibe from Manny. Do you?"

Britton looked at me, and her face said everything that needed to be said. She felt the same way as Owen, and I couldn't understand why. It's not like he's done something to lose my trust. I've read his file and see that he's a ladies man, but when you're *that* fine, it's understandable.

"Just be safe, Ani."

"No. Tell me why you think he has ulterior motives? Is it because a man like that wouldn't want a woman like me?"

"Ani, it's not like that at all. I'm just saying that he showed interest in you rather quickly. We both know that he's out here slanging dick left and right, and for him to all of a sudden want to settle down and take things seriously with you is suspect to me. I don't trust anyone these days, especially since you've come into your own as a cartel boss. I'm not trying to stop you from seeing him. I just want you to be safe."

A part of me could appreciate where she was coming from. However, I still felt like she was insinuating something else.

"Thanks for looking out for me, but I can handle myself." I tried to fake like I wasn't slightly hurt. Britton knows me well enough to know when I'm faking, yet she didn't call me out on it.

My phone rang, breaking the awkward silence between us. Manny was letting me know that he was outside. I kissed Britton goodbye and walked out of my room. My mom was seated on the couch with a cup of tea in her hand with her legs crossed.

"Have a good night, Ms. Mack," was all I said as I continued to the front door.

"He can't come in and meet your mother? What kind of man is that, Ani? And why are you wearing such a tight dress? Can you breathe?" She fired off question after question. She was more nervous about this date than I was.

"Ma, this ain't that yet. I don't know what's to come of this situation. If a man meets my mother, then he's lucky. Manny isn't that lucky, at least not yet. Also, this dress looks banging on my body." I twirled in a slow circle for her to see. "Ever since you put me through hell with training, my body's been looking right and tight. Now, if you'll excuse me, I gotta get going. Don't want to keep him waiting too long. I'll tell you all about it in the morning. You have yourself a great evening. Don't be up all night waiting on Kindred to call." I smirked at her, and she shooed me out the door.

She didn't think I knew, but she's been up to the prison a lot more than she's lead on. Plus, I could hear the late-night conversations. She wasn't fooling anyone but herself. Kindred Edwards has her heart, and there was no changing that. He and I haven't spoken yet, in all honesty, I wasn't ready for that, not yet at least.

"Don't get cute, Ani! I can still whoop you!" she yelled at me as I shut the door to the house.

When I looked outside, Manny was leaning against a snow white Bentley truck, pretty impressive ride for a first date. White must have been his favorite color since he was dressed in it from head to toe, along with more jewelry than I've ever seen on one person. I've never been the flashy type, so this didn't impress me too much.

He saw me walking down the stairs and licked his lips while swiped his hand down his face— typical hood nigga shit. Owen was standing by the fleet of black trucks waiting for a move to be made. I didn't want him trailing behind us, but apparently, he had to do it. He assured me that we wouldn't even know he was there.

"Gal, com' 'ere." His accent got me every time he opened his mouth. I giggled as I stepped up to him and he twirled me in a circle. "Damn." I guess that was his way of approving my outfit.

"Are you going to stand there gawking at me or are we going to go enjoy this night?" He nodded and opened the car door.

The peanut butter colored seats looked even better in person. They were smooth, and I instantly melted in them as he closed my door. Before I got too lost in the seat, I reached over and unlocked his door.

"I see ya 'ave manners. Ya moms raised ya right." Yeah, Mariyah Mack raised me with some kind of manners.

"What do you have planned for the evening?"

He just smiled with those gold teeth and continued to drive. I had no idea what he had planned, but I was down for the ride.

❂

THIS NIGHT WITH MANNY WAS GOING BY SMOOTHLY, AND honestly, I didn't want it to end. He wasn't from Chicago and wanted to play like he was a tourist. We did a nighttime bus tour, ate deep dish pizza, and even visited Navy Pier. All in all, we had a great day.

We were currently cruising down Lake Shore Drive admiring the city lights. This city had a lot going on, but one couldn't deny her beauty. Her beauty outshined anything else being said about her. I don't know what else he had planned for the night, yet I was down for whatever, at least that's what I thought.

The car came to a stop, and we were pulling up to the Ritz Carlton. Panic started to set in, and I prayed that he was only stopping here to meet up with a friend. We hadn't discussed sex yet, and I had been avoiding it at all costs. It's not that I'm not ready for it. It's just that I'm not ready to take that step with *him*.

"Chill out. We can sleep in separate rooms if you want. I'm just tryna chill with ya some more. We can order snacks and watch movies."

Against my better judgment, I exited the car, and we walked hand in hand to the front desk. Thankfully, he got us separate rooms and got us checked in.

"What am I going to do about clothes?"

"Ya, detail is still 'round right?" I forgot that Owen wasn't too far behind.

"Yes, let me get situated, and then I'll be down." He nodded, and we went to our separate floors. His room was one floor under mine, and I appreciated that. It gave me a sense of privacy.

This room was something out of a dream. He had set me up with a king size suite, and it was much more space than I needed. I started to walk around the room to see what all it had to offer. It was gorgeous and had everything that I would need. A knock on the door startled me. Hesitantly, I opened it and came nose to nose with Owen. His face was stone cold while his eyes told another story. Something was troubling him.

"Everything okay?" I asked him. He just nodded and waited for me to say something else. "Well, it looks like I'm going to chill here with Manny for a while. I don't have any clothes with me. Would you mind stopping by the house and getting some things for me? Wait...I'll text Britton to pack me a bag. Can you just grab it from her? And there's no rush on you getting back here. I'm fine, no one knows I'm here, and Manny isn't a threat."

Again, he nodded without any words and left out of the room. I'm not sure what his problem was, but he needed to get his shit together.

❧ 19 ❧

OWEN PIERCE

YESTERDAY

Lately, I had been staying in the room that Ms. Mack offered me at Ani's estate. Camille and I haven't been seeing things eye to eye since the night we spoke on having kids. She also wasn't feelin' the fact that my new job had me away from her all the time. The bigger Ani's name got, the longer hours I had to work in order to keep her safe. Her life had been threatened on more than one occasion lately, and that helped me step my game up. I had been hitting the gym hard whenever I had some downtime, and the work was paying off.

"Hey old man, how you feelin' today?"

My pops was still allowin' his pride get the best of him. He had yet to tell me what's really going on with him. His cough was getting worse, and I promised that I would go see him on my next day off.

"Hey Owen," he spoke groggily in the phone. Usually, he would go off on me about calling him old, but today he let it slide. He wasn't feeling like himself, and it was killin' me that I hadn't made time for him.

"You need me to come chill with you or take you to the doctor?"

"No, continue to do what you're doing. I'm going to be fine, Owen." His coughing fit started again. It hurt like hell to know that the man that raised you doesn't want you to help him. "Owen, I'm proud of you son. I know that you've had a rough life and things didn't always work out the way that we thought *they would. However, you are coming into your own. I know what you do out there for Tony, and I want you to be safe. Get ready for work, and I'll talk to you later."*

The coughing started once again, and before I could say anything, he hung up the phone. I hated that he didn't trust me enough to tell me what's bothering him. We've always had an open relationship, and I don't know what changed. I need to find time to pay him a visit.

PRESENT DAY

I didn't think Ani hanging with Emmanuel would bother me as much as it did. I'd been around here long enough to see that behind this cartel shit, she was a soft and gentle person. Manny wasn't the type of guy she needed in her life. He was too into himself to see her true beauty. However, it wasn't my place to say anything to her. I wasn't the type of nigga to sneak diss another. She'd find out about him soon enough.

As I drove back to the estate, my mind drifted to my pops. I hadn't had much free time while on the job, and his house was on the way. On the way over there, I received a call from Camille. I had half a mind not to even pay attention to it, but if I didn't answer she wasn't going to stop.

"Owen, baby, you need to get to Christ Hospital. It's your father." I heard what she said yet the shit wasn't registering. "Owen, hello? Are you there?" I hung up the phone and hit the dash all the way to the hospital.

The car came to a screeching halt when I pulled in front of the hospital. I didn't give a fuck about it getting towed. At this moment the only thing that mattered to me was my father. The world outside of him didn't exist.

"Hey, I'm here to see about my father, Henry Pierce."

The nurse at the station quickly typed in his name and found his information. She gave me a visitor's pass, and I ran all the way to his room.

When I walked into the room, I lost the air in my lungs, and the walls were closing in on me. My rock, for the past twenty-eight years, was lying in bed not hooked up to any machines. His eyes were closed, and the bed wasn't propped up like normal. The ashy grayness of his skin let me know that my main man was gone.

Tucked away in the corner of the room silently sobbing was Camille. The fact that she was here at the hospital before me ignited a fire within me. How the hell did she beat me here? How did she know that my pops was in trouble?

"Owen!" she cried out. Her head was previously in her hands, but when she heard me walk in the room, she immediately popped up. "I'm so sorry." She walked towards me, and I backed up. I couldn't handle her touching me right now.

"No, nah." My brain was having an even harder time registering everything. This was all too much. "How did he die?"

"I don't know. He called me earlier today and said that he wanted to clear the air with me. He let me know that he gives me his blessing to marry you. Owen, he said that he's always cared for me but was too stubborn to admit it. I-I'm so sorry." She sobbed on the floor in front of me. I sat in the chair dumbfounded. My father was really gone. This shit was so surreal.

"Excuse me, are you Owen Pierce?" A short woman with silver hair and a white coat walked in the room and closed the door behind her.

"Y-yeah," I whimpered. I hadn't cried in a long ass time, and for some reason, when she closed the door, I started bawling. The doctor wrapped her arms around me and held onto me while I cried.

"My name is Dr. Young, and I've been working with your father for quite some time. It's going to be okay, son."

Hearing this woman confirm my worst nightmare ignited a fire in me. Why didn't he just tell me what was going on with him? If I had known, then maybe I could have helped!

"He knew that if you found out about his condition, then you would have put your life on hold, dear. Henry's told me all about you Owen and the things that you've gone through. He knew that you would have dropped everything you're doing to take care of him, and he didn't want that."

"H-how did he die? Is it hereditary? Is it something that could affect our future children? I want to know everything." The doctor stopped consoling me for a moment to look at Camille.

"I'm sorry and who are *you*?" she questioned with sass in her voice.

"I'm Camille, Owen's soon to be fiancée." She held out her hand, and the doctor sized her up.

"I'm sorry love, but I don't know you, so therefore I can't discuss patient information with you. The emergency contact only read Owen Pierce, and from the looks of it, you are not him. Now if he decides to tell you what happened then, that's his prerogative. However, right now, I'm going to need you to step outside while I talk to the family in private." She walked to the door and held it open.

Camille's face was filled with confusion. She didn't know what to think of the doctor's outburst. Before she could say anything, my phone rang. Ani was calling and I'm sure she was just trying to figure out when I was coming back with her clothes.

"Yeah," I answered. I tried to hide the fact that I had been crying. I waited for a response but didn't get one. "Ani, you there?"

"C-can you come back please?" She spoke so low that I had barely heard her. My antennas went up, and I immediately feared the worse.

"Ani? Ani, talk to me. Tell me what's wrong?" The doctor looked at me with a face of worry. This day was getting worse by the minute. "Ani, I need you to talk to me. Tell me what's going on. I can't help you if you don't tell me."

"Who the hell is Ani?" I waved Camille off. "Owen answer me!" She demanded through gritted teeth. Ani still hadn't answered me, and it was pissing me off. I had to choose between grieving and my job.

"Ani, give me twenty minutes, and I'll be there." I turned towards the doctor, and she held her hand up.

"Here's my card, dear. You come find me once you get *that* situation under control. The morgue is on the way to take the body. You can make the arrangements with them tomorrow. Now get going." I thanked her for her generosity and started running down the hall to the elevator.

"Owen, I need you to tell me what's going on. You're leaving me in the dark, and it's not right. I have a right to know what's going on."

"It's work, Camille. I told you when I started this damn job that shit wasn't going to be simple."

"Who is Ani? Is she the other woman?"

"No, I can't answer any more of your questions. This is wasting precious time. I gotta go. I'll talk to you later." I shook my head at her and took the stairs all the way down. Thankfully, the car was still parked outside, and I was able to hop in and head back to the hotel.

Speeding down the highway, I hated that I left Ani by herself with Emmanuel. On the other hand, I was fighting back tears. The man that raised me and taught me everything I knew was gone. This shit was far too much for me to handle. I opened the car door before I came to a complete stop. I couldn't get to her fast enough. Ani never called my phone for help, so I knew this was serious.

When I arrived at her door, I remembered that I didn't have a key card. She was going to have to let me in.

"Ani, open up." I placed my ear against the door, and the only thing that I could hear was soft sobs. "Ani, baby, I need you to open the door. I don't have a key." The word "baby" rolled off my tongue effortlessly, and I didn't even mind.

After a few minutes, the door creaked open, and I flew in. Ani was in the middle of the suite wrapped in a bloodstained sheet with tears running down her face. I ran through the room to see if there was a body or blood. I needed some kind of clue as to what happened.

"Ani," I kneeled in front of her and held her face in my hands. Her eyes were red, and snot ran from her nose. Her beautiful cocoa skin was puffy and pale. "Tell me what happened." She slowly turned around and dropped the sheet off her shoulders to off her body to reveal what she was hiding.

20

ANI MACK

I didn't know who to call in this situation. Britton was out of the question because she was going to come in here acting a fool. My mother would freak out and cry all day, and I didn't need that right now. I needed someone who would be able to harbor the same anger as me. Owen was the perfect person. His nonchalant demeanor probably came off *soft* to others, but to me, I knew that he was battling some inner demons. The anger was there for him, and that's the shit that I needed right now.

"You ready to tell me what happened?" Owen held my chin up and our eyes locked. I wasn't ready to tell anyone what happened, yet with him, I felt comfortable enough doing so.

AN HOUR BEFORE

Once Owen left to get my things, I made my way to Manny's room one floor down. It's been a long time since I've chilled with a man, and I didn't know what to expect. I just wanted to chill and not be "Ani, the Cartel Boss". Was that too much to ask?

When I made it to his room, I knocked and waited for him to answer the door. It took him a few minutes, and when he opened the door, I could see why.

Clouds of smoke filled the air and blew into the hallway. I had no idea that he was a smoker. I didn't want to assume, but most drug dealers puffed on gas every once in a while. The smoking didn't bother me, so I walked in and kicked my heels off.

In his suite area, he had a bunch of snacks set up and the TV set to Netflix. I've never been one to be nervous around men. However, when I'm around him, I feel like a little schoolgirl. When my shoes were off, I plopped down on the couch and picked up a bag of chips.

As I searched through Netflix, Manny came walking into the room with only white sweat pants hanging off his hips. His chest was sculpted nicely and covered in tattoos. He was a darker complexion like me, therefore making it hard for me to analyze the ink. Once I was able to take my eyes off the ink, I began taking in the rest of his appearance. His dreads were pulled into a ball at the top of his head, and his eyes hung low. Those gold teeth made their appearance, and I couldn't help but smile.

"Come on. Let's watch this movie." I patted the space next to me, and he plopped down on the couch. The movie started, and I laid my head on his shoulder.

Before the opening scene could start, I felt his hand in my hair, and he was pushing my head down towards his lap. I laughed it off and swatted his hand away. Again, I laid my head on his shoulder, but this time he pushed my head down further into his lap. With his free hand, he released his penis from his pants and tried to place my mouth near it. Manny was a lot stronger than me, and it was a struggle to fight him.

"What are you doing?" I asked as I squirmed out of his grasp.

"Just kiss it, gal. Ya know ya want to." He was one cocky sick bastard, and I refuse to be pressured into anything. Yes, we had a good vibe between us. However, I wasn't ready for that with him.

"No!" I moved his hand out of the way and tried to stand up from the couch. I wasn't moving quickly enough as he grabbed a hand full of my hair and swung me down on the couch.

'Com' back 'ere!" he roared.

I guess rejection wasn't something that Manny was used to but to today was a different day and I was a different woman. I don't know what he thought, but this wasn't that.

"I'm advising you to stop and let my hair go," I urged, but it fell on deaf ears.

He pulled my dress, and it ripped into shreds, releasing my breasts and revealing the thin piece of lace tucked away between my ass cheeks. I began clawing at his arms in an attempt to get him to release my hair. With all of my strength, I pushed him back, and his head bounced off the wall. He was in a daze. However, that only lasted a few moments. He shook it off and then lunged at me with all of his might. As quickly as I could, I hit him with two punches to his face causing him to fly backwards onto the floor. While he was figuring out what happened, I ran towards the door in an attempt to escape. However, he was able to grab my ankle, and my face came crashing down on to the floor. Blood leaked from my face like a running faucet and covered the white marble floor. My body was growing weary from the beating, but I couldn't give up on myself, not today, not ever. I tried getting out of his grasp by kicking his arm, but he was too strong. He was then able to slide me back towards him, and he straddled me.

The look in his eyes was demonic, and I just knew that nothing would be the same. I had allowed this man to come into my life in hopes that he was a good guy, yet, he proved me wrong. Men like him only saw one thing when it came to me— pussy. He was trash like the rest of them, and I'll be damned if I let him get what he wanted.

He was still on top of me fondling my breasts as I cried and whimpered. His nails dug into my skin as he roughly inserted two fingers into my vagina. My body was hurting in every way possible. Instead of me giving in and allowing this abuse to continue, I quickly began thinking of ways to get from under him and out of here. That's when my mind drifted to the training classes with my mother. She had taught us how to get out of situations similar to this one.

Manny placed his hand around my throat, and with the back of my arm, I brought it in front of his and delivered several blows to his face with my elbow. The impact and pain caused him to fall backward and hold his face in agony. Unfortunately, for him, I wasn't stopping there. He needed to know that I wasn't one to fuck with. I ran towards him and rained down punch after punch. Everything that I had been holding back was being unleashed on him. I was sick and tired, and I wasn't stopping any time soon. Blood spewed everywhere, and I didn't care. I grabbed one of my high-heeled shoes and connected it with his face, over and over and over again until my body gave out and his chest stopped moving in and out.

As I stood to my feet, examining the damage I had done, I wondered where

I was supposed to go from here. This excessive force was going to be hard to explain. I needed to get out of this room and call for some help. Situations like these called for a special set of people, and I knew just who to contact.

For now, I needed to get back to my room. I grabbed a sheet out of the bedroom and wrapped it around my body. I opened the door slightly and looked both ways to make sure that the coast was clear. I'm sure there were cameras in the hallways, and that's something that I'll need to take care of later. I made it to the elevator and back to my room without anyone noticing me.

Once the door was closed, and locked tears ran down my face. This was far too much for me to handle right now. I knew I needed to call someone for help.

"Hey Timbs, I need you at the Ritz."

I proceeded to give him all of the information, and he assured me that everything would be okay. He and his crew would handle everything from the cleanup to the law, and even the security tapes. I appreciated having efficient people on the payroll.

Once I hung up with him, I decided to call for help. Britton and my mother were completely out of the question. They would freak out and ask too many questions. I didn't need that right now. The only thing I needed was for someone to come sit with me who wasn't going to judge me or say too many words.

"That's when I called you." I looked up at Owen and rage filled his eyes along with a hint of sorrow. "Please, don't feel sorry for me. I'm okay."

"That's not it. It's just—" He held his head down and took a deep breath. Obviously, my situation wasn't the only thing on his mind.

"What's wrong, Owen? Talk to me."

A tear slid down his face, and my heart started to hurt for him. I've never seen him show emotions. He was always stone-faced, so this was something new for me.

"My pops passed away tonight. It's just a lot to deal with." When he said that, my heart stopped. He was going through the pain of losing a parent, and yet he was here trying to console me.

"Owen, no." I hung my head in shame. I would have never called him for help if I had known. His situation was much more important than mine was. "I'm so sorry. Have you started making any arrangements?"

He shook his head. It was far too early in the morning for anything to be done, but as soon as nine a.m. hit, we were going to take care of his father. I found myself wrapping my arms around him to comfort him, and it came as a shock to both of us. He held his head up and began to search my eyes for some kind of answer. The look that he gave me made me feel self-conscious.

Just as we were both caught up in the moment, my phone dinged, and it was Timbs alerting me that everything was in motion. They would be done within the hour. I thanked him and let him know that payment would be processed shortly. By this time, Owen had released me from his gaze.

"I'm truly sorry, Owen. Unfortunately, I don't know what it's like to lose a parent, so I can't tell you how to feel right now. Honestly, I'm in no shape to give anyone any advice right now."

"It's all good. I don't expect you to," he stated while wiping his face with the back of his hand. Tears had been falling down his face, and it was killing me softly.

Owen and I didn't know much about each other, but somehow, there was chemistry between us. In this moment, on this floor, wrapped in a bloody sheet, I found myself wanting to know everything about Owen Pierce. I wanted to know his favorite color, what makes him laugh, what makes him cry? I wanted to know what his childhood was like and how life had been treating him so far.

My eyes traveled over him, and I began taking in everything about him that I had missed before. From his golden colored skin, his perfectly round baldhead, down to the scattered freckles on his face, Owen was as handsome as they come. His face normally wore a scowl, but right now, it held pain. It housed fear and hurt, and the only thing that I wanted to do was take the pain away.

"Who are you?" The words came out of my mouth and his eyes focused in on me. His lips parted as if he was going to say something, but that never came. Instead, he hung his head and shrugged his shoulders.

"Owen, who are you?" I asked again in hopes that he would cooperate this time.

"I'm nobody." He shook his head and wiped his face one more time while getting up from the floor.

"Come on, Ani. We need to get you showered."

Owen touched my arm, and I flinched. The gesture quickly reminding me of everything I had been through tonight. He held his hands up in surrender and gave me a minute to collect myself. I was beginning to feel hopeless and helpless. I couldn't even help through his issues because I was slowly losing my own mind.

"Ani, don't worry about me. We gotta get you cleaned up, and then you need to rest. It's been a tripped-out night for both of us."

I finally placed my hand in his, and he helped me stand to my feet. Every part of my body ached, and I just wanted to cry. We made our way to the bathroom, hand in hand, and I began to realize that this was the closest that the two of us had been.

He led me to the oversized tub and told me to have a seat on the ledge. Once I sat down, he reached over, turned on the faucet, and poured the lavender scented bubble bath into the water. Was he going to stay in here and help me bathe? My heart began beating out of my chest at the very thought of it. He held his hand out for me to take again, and I extended my trembling arm. As I stood up from the ledge, I got weak in the knees and almost collapsed on the floor. He grabbed me just in time and held on to me while looking in my eyes. It felt like we were staring at each other for an eternity when he finally pulled his eyes away from mine.

"Watch your step," he lectured as I stepped into the scolding hot water.

On a normal day, I would hate for my water to be this hot. However, in this moment, I wanted it hotter than it was. I wanted to be able to melt any trace of Manny off my body. My body didn't deserve any remnants of Emmanuel.

"Here," Owen spoke to me, snapping me out of my fury while handing me a washcloth and bar of soap. "I'll be standing on the other side of the door if you need anything." I started to protest, but he was already shutting the door behind him.

The sound of the door closing caused the floodgates to open. I had been crying uncontrollably since all of this took place, and there was no stopping these damn tears. Manny had broken me in the worst way possible. In one night, I had been the victim of attempted rape as well as adding another murder to my list. The burden of being a cartel boss was becoming too much to bear. Just the thought of what my life would have been like if I hadn't accepted this position caused my silent sobs to transform into full-blown screams of terror.

"Why me, Lord? Why me?" I cried out. "Please take this pain away from me. I don't want it anymore!"

I slowly began submerging myself into the water and letting it cover me. The water welcomed me like a lost child gone for too long. It embraced me, and I accepted the warmth. As I began to relax, I could hear the door to the bathroom opening, and my body was pulled up from the water.

"Don't you ever let a nigga make you feel this low, Ani! Fuck that nigga and everything that he stands for!" Owen had jumped in the tub with me and was now cradling me in his arms.

"I-I'm sorry!" I sobbed. "I just don't know where to go from here! Where do I go from here, Owen?"

"You go forward, Ani. When life pushes you back, baby you continue to fight and push forward. Do you understand me?" He took his thumbs and wiped away the tears while placing a small kiss on my forehead. "Ani, I just lost the only person that ever loved me. Don't you think that I want to give up? Of course, I do, but what good is that going to do? I can't make my old man proud if I become a 'nothing ass nigga'. Instead, I'm going to continue to fight and live the life that he wanted for me."

Instead of stepping out of the tub, he sat down in the water and pulled me into his embrace. "You asked me who I am..." he took a long pause and proceeded to finish. "I'm just another black man that got the short end of the stick. A few years back, I was arrested on felony robbery charges. I ended up being in the wrong place at the wrong time and to make a long story short. I ended up with jail time. My public defender was so swamped with his caseload that he didn't even know my name or the case he was supposed to be defending me on. Cook County locked my ass up and hasn't thought twice about me since."

"Owen—"

"Nah shorty, don't start feeling sorry for me. I gave up on feeling sorry for myself a long time ago. Instead, I worked my ass off at the one job I could find until a better opportunity came my way."

I looked up at him and a small smile formed on his face. He was talking about me and his job as my bodyguard.

Seeing the small smile on his face did something to me. It caused every worry that I was currently facing to disappear without a trace. If he could do this to me with just a smile, there's no telling what else he could accomplish.

Silence filled the room as our eyes searched one another. I had taken in some of his facial features. However, I wanted to know and see everything there was. From his thick pink lips and perfectly sculpted jawline that flexed every now and then, to how his nostrils flared in and out every time he took a deep breath.

Owen wasn't letting up either. His eyes moved slowly over my face as he pulled off the curly strands of wet hair stuck to my face. As he looked over me, I saw the seriousness return to his face.

"You're fuckin' gorgeous."

It's a simple compliment. However, it meant everything to me. With my hand, I caressed the side of his face. For a brief moment, he closed his eyes and pulled his bottom lip into his mouth.

21

BRITTON MATTHEWS

I hadn't heard from Ani all night, and I was dying to hear the details of her date. She and Manny were going strong, and I wanted to hear everything. I texted her phone last night, and I have yet to receive a response. That's unusual for her because we all know her phone is practically attached to her, but I guess I'll chalk it up to her having a good time. She'll call me when she's ready. I had other things to worry about.

My assistant Paisley snapped her fingers at me to get my attention. She had been running down my schedule for the day, and I hadn't heard a word she said. It wasn't that what she was saying wasn't important. It's just that I had a lot on my mind. Between everything going on with Ani, and everything going on with DJ, I had little time to worry about anything else.

Speaking of DJ, he's decided to take some time away from me since I told him to earn me. There were a few ways that I could take this. Either he was doing everything he could to make things right on his end before he approached me, or he ran away from my ultimatum. My heart started to beat rapidly when I thought about him leaving me. Truth be told, I hated every second that we were apart. DJ had a hold on my heart, and there was no escaping it. One minute I loved him, and then the next minute I hated him.

"Britton, are you even listening to me?" I nodded at her even though I hadn't heard a word she said. She gave me a knowing look and shook her head. "Range is here early. I was trying to prepare you for that, but your head's been in the clouds today. Do you want me to reschedule? I can say an emergency came up." She pointed at the security monitor that showed Range arriving.

"Sorry, I just have a lot on my mind. No need to reschedule, I'm just going to get this over with and hopefully it'll be fine. But from the way that he's walking, he's about to add to my stress."

This cocky muthafucka walked in the gym like his name was on the lease. Damn near every woman that was in there had their mouths wide open. His sex appeal was alluring, but I knew the man behind the body. He was an egotistical and narcissistic pig.

"Let's get this shit over with," I mumbled under my breath as Paisley and I walked out of my office. She snickered and tried to hold in the rest of her laugh. "Keep it up, and I'll return the Chanel bag I got you." She straightened herself up and walked back to her desk.

"Love you, Brit!" she yelled after me. In return, I stuck up my middle finger and made my way over to Range.

"Good afternoon, Britton." Range walked over to me and tried to hug me. I stopped him with my arm and held my hand out to shake his. "Oh, we're not hugging. Okay, I can respect that."

"Let's get started."

I needed to be quick and to the point with him. I didn't want him thinking that this was anything other than what we had agreed upon. Range had a banging ass body, and he did *not* need my help, whatsoever. Despite the fact that I didn't want to be here with him, I was able to get a good workout in.

***

"Good job today. Remember to sign out with Paisley. I'll see you at your next session." I turned around to walk away from him, but he stopped me when he grabbed my arm and pulled me closer to him.

"Let me take you to lunch. It's the least I can do after that work-out." He pulled me up closer to him and placed his ashy ass lips on my cheek.

"The only thanks that I need is your credit card processing success-fully." I pried my arm from his grip. "Have a good day, Range."

"You know I don't take well to rejection Britton. I get what I want," he urged.

"Are you willing to die on that hill?"

He had no idea of the dangerous game he was playing. If DJ and I continued to work on things, then Range would find himself in a whole world of trouble. I didn't have time to have his death on my conscience.

"For you? Yeah, I'm willing to die on that hill." His words had me stuck as he signed out and walked out of the building.

The sun had gone down, and darkness had fallen by the time I finished up with my clients. I still hadn't heard from Ani, and I wanted nothing more than to make sure that she was good. I tried Owen's cell, but I didn't get a response. Both of them being off the grid had my antennas up.

I quickly locked up the gym and made my way to my car. I needed to get to Mariyah and see if we could track their location. My heart raced as I fumbled through my purse for my keys.

"Excuse me, Ms. Britton. Can I have a word with you?"

I quickly turned around to see who was calling my name. It turns out it was Nolton. My heart was in my throat, and I needed to catch my breath. Sneaking up on me like that was sure to give me a damn heart attack.

"Sup, Nolton? What you doing over here?"

"Hey um, you know where I can find Ani?" He had his hands in his pockets while swaying back and forth.

"Nah, actually I haven't heard from her today. I'm gonna go find her though. When I hear from her, I'll tell her to give you a call."

I turned around to open my car door, but I was quickly thrown against the car. A knife was placed at my throat, and it was on the verge of breaking my skin. Tears streamed down my face as I silently prayed that this wasn't the end for me.

"Stop with all that damn crying. You know just as well as I know that Ani doesn't deserve this shit! This was supposed to be mine. Your little friend came around and took what was mine. Give her a message for me next time you see her," he pressed the knife deeper into my skin, and I immediately felt the blood dripping down my neck. "Let her know that I won't stop until she's dead and gone. Everyone one of you muthafuckas is going to suffer until Ani is gone."

He pushed off me and ran off into the night while I grabbed something to stop the bleeding on my neck. I jumped in my car and made sure to lock the door. I've dealt with a lot of shit in my past when it came to this game, but never anything like this. I needed to find Ani and make sure that she was okay. Before I could do that, I needed to calm myself down.

"Hello," DJ's voice rang out through my speakers, and I instantly burst into tears. I started crying uncontrollably and couldn't get the words out. "Aye bae, talk to me. What's wrong? Britton, I can't help you if you don't tell me what's going on."

"H-he's going to kill Ani!"

"Wait, who's gonna kill Ani? Fuck that where you at? Are you at the gym?"

"Yes," I cried into the phone.

"I'm not too far stay there? You strapped?" I nodded, but then realized that he couldn't see me.

"Yes."

He hung up the phone and made it to me within fifteen minutes. Seeing him step out of his car and run to me had my heart beating out of my chest. He swung the door open and checked me out. He saw the cut on my neck, and his face immediately changed.

"I'm fine, I promise. I just overreacted a little bit. I'm good," I tried to reassure him, yet he wasn't falling for it.

"Nah, come on get in my car. We'll have someone come and get it. We need to get you checked out." He helped me to the car and sped off into the night. "Here, take this and apply pressure." He handed me a fresh towel after he saw that the current one was soaked in blood.

"Hey, I need you. Meet me at the loft," he spoke into the phone. I didn't know that he had a loft here in Chicago. I had assumed that he was living out of a hotel. His whole life was back in Philly. I was puzzled at this point.

After a few minutes, the car came to a stop in front of a parking garage. We had arrived at an extravagant building in downtown. When I got a better look at it, I noticed that this was the same building that I had been wanting to move into for the longest. There hadn't been any vacancies in months, I don't know how he scored a place in here, but I was going to make it my mission to find out.

The garage door opened, and he pulled in with ease. Once the car was parked, he came over and helped me out. The way that he was catering to me right now made me want to give him everything that I had. Those old feelings that I had concealed were resurfacing, and I was starting to realize why I fell in love with him in the first place.

Dorian was everything that a woman could ask for— charming, sophisticated, loving, and a protector. There wasn't a day that went by when he didn't give me what I *needed* out of a man. The only thing that stopped me from taking his last name was the fact that he wasn't letting up on this drug game. At times, it seemed that he loved it more than he loved me. That was a problem.

I guess my inner feelings were showing on my face as we rode the elevator up to the penthouse. He stood in front of me with a scowl on his face. It was as if he was trying to read my mind and figure out what was making me sad. Everything that happened today was starting to weigh in on me. I still hadn't heard from Ani, hearing Range tell me that he was going to die trying to get me, Nolton trying to kill me, and now I was in an elevator with the man that had my heart in the palm of his hands.

He looked at me and started to open his mouth, but the elevator doors opened. On the other side, in the massive ass foyer stood a woman in a white coat, with a slinky black dress, and six-inch heels. She smiled when she saw DJ. That smile went away as quickly as it came when I stepped from behind him.

"Hey, thanks for comin' on such short notice."

He walked up to her and hugged her. It was the kind of hug that you give to someone after not seeing them for quite some time. The shit had my attention, and I didn't know whether I should stay in the room or get back on the elevator. I finally decided to just step to the side while they spoke in hushed tones. Whatever he said to her caused her attitude to change, and she looked past him, sizing me up. After she sized me up, an eye roll followed the look, and I was ready to knock her head off her shoulders. DJ must have felt me walking towards him. He quickly turned around to face me. Barbie walked away, set her bag down on the kitchen island, and started pulling stuff out with an attitude.

I didn't have time for this shit. The cut on my neck wasn't that deep, and I could walk into any emergency room and get it handled. I called for the elevator and pulled out my phone to call an Uber. DJ and this unknown bitch had me fucked up if they thought I was going to stand here and take this funky ass attitude.

"Britton, bring yo ass back here so that she can look at your neck!" he yelled from behind.

"Fuck you and that bitch. I saw the way she looked at me, and I'll kill a bitch dead before she disrespects me like that again!"

The elevator dinged and the doors opened. Before I could move an inch, I was being picked up and put over his shoulder.

"Put me down, nigga. I'm not gonna accept disrespect from no nigga or bitch on God's green earth. I've had enough for one day. I promise you I have!"

"Sit yo ass down and stop all this bullshit. This is Skylar, my damn sister. Let her take a look at yo damn neck, and then the three of us are going to have a conversation," he spoke through gritted teeth as he placed me in a chair.

My mouth was wide open when he revealed that she was his sister. DJ and I dated for a while, and I can't remember anything about him having a sister.

"It's a long story, Britton. I'll explain everything in a minute." Skylar came over and removed the napkin from my neck. After a few minutes, she cleaned up the wound and gave me three stitches.

"Done," she said while disposing of her gloves.

"Um, thank you. I'm sorry about earlier." I held out my hand for her to shake. She hesitated, but eventually, she shook it.

"No problem, I understand how it looks. My little brother and I haven't seen each other in a very long time. When I graduated from medical school, I decided to broaden my horizons and head to Africa. My services were needed over there a lot more than they were here."

"Yeah, baby sis is a beast with this medical shit!" he yelled out from the other room. "She's been over there serving her country and taking care of the less fortunate."

"Why'd you never tell me about her?" I had been sitting here this whole time, racking my brain to see if DJ ever mentioned her.

"Her safety."

In a sense that was completely understandable, but I wasn't just anybody. I was his woman, who at the time was going to be his wife. I can't even sit here and lie. My feelings were hurt. Did he not trust me enough with this information?

"Aye, stop thinkin' so much on it. No one could know because of her status at the time. She's a government official, Brit."

"You mean to tell me you're the biggest drug dealer on the east coast and your sister works for the fuckin' government?"

"Now you see why I didn't tell you. It's not that I didn't want to. I literally couldn't for her safety."

"Well, I'm going to leave you two love birds—"

"No, wait. I'm not done asking questions. Why did you have an attitude when you saw me? You don't know me, and you're judging me?" DJ took a deep breath and slowly let it out. He knew that I wasn't going to let this go until I had answers.

"I apologize for that, Britton. It's just that I've heard so much about you and how much my baby brother loves you. Then for him to tell me that you two are no longer together pissed me off. From what I've heard, you two love each other past the moon and the stars. Try to make it work, Britton, he's worth it. And I'm not just saying that because he's my brother." She came over to hug me and then handed me a piece of paper. "This is for the pain. Take care. I hope to see you soon, under *different* circumstances."

I thanked her for her help, and she took the elevator down.

Once she left, an awkward silence filled the air. DJ stood next to the refrigerator with his arms folded. He looked as if he wanted to say something, but my phone rang before he could get the chance to.

"We have a situation," Tony said from the other side of the phone. This night wasn't getting any better.

❧ 22 ❧

OWEN PIERCE

Camille had been blowing my phone up nonstop since I walked out of the hospital yesterday. I don't know what kinda nigga she thought she was fuckin' with when she gave me an ultimatum. I didn't do those, and I damn sure wasn't gonna do it with a bitch that thought that I was gonna cave into her demands. That ain't me, and will never be me. The only person that had the luxury of tellin' me what the fuck to do was Ani, and we weren't even on the same page right now. I didn't mean for shit to go as far as it did, but there was no going back. What's done is done, and hopefully, we could move on and not change anything.

Everything from last night was a complete blur. With my pops passing, my whole world had been turned upside down. I had no one left in this world, and the shit rocked me to the core. The only thing that wasn't a blur was how far Ani and I had taken things. Subconsciously, I knew that I had feelings for her. I just didn't know how deep they ran. Being in her *true* presence had me feeling some kind of way. I don't even know how to explain it.

I had to get out of my head, or this was going to eat me alive. Ani and I were on two different levels, and we could never be together. She's the head of a fuckin' cartel, and I'm just the bodyguard. A relationship between the two of us wouldn't be in her best interest. We could get distracted, and she could lose her life at the hands of our love. That's not what I wanted for her.

Instead of focusing on us, I needed to focus on the task at hand. We were currently at the funeral home making arrangements for my father. When I returned to the hotel this morning after getting us some new clothes, Ani told me that we needed to talk. I thought we were going to discuss last night, but she explained how she wanted to help me plan my father's funeral. She felt the need to do this since I wasn't able to speak to him one last time due to her cry for help. I tried over and over to tell her that it wasn't necessary. However, I learned that she's not a person that I can say no to.

On the car ride over here, we had fussed and fought about what kind of home going he should have. I wanted to have a simple memorial, and Ani wanted extravagant shit. I can hear her in my head now. *Owen, your father deserves to go out in style. That's the least I can do. I refuse to let you burn him and dump his ashes in Lake Michigan! Nope, that's not going to work for me.* That's about all she said to me. Other than a few minutes of conversation about the arrangements, we stayed completely silent.

"Thank you, Clarke. I truly appreciate all of your help," Ani said as she spoke with the funeral director. We'd spent a good amount of our day running around the city, and I was exhausted. I honestly wouldn't have made it through this stuff without her.

Once they finished, she decided that it was time to head home. The silence on the way back to the estate was killing me. Last night was something different, and I think that it scared both of us. Feelings were now involved. It's not as if we talked much before, but I couldn't deal with this awkward shit.

"Are you hungry?" I asked while we drove down the expressway. Instead of giving me a verbal response, she shifted in her seat and turned her face to look outside the window. "I know you're hungry, Ani. I can hear your stomach growling. Ani, I know you hear me."

This time, she pulled her AirPods out of her bag and placed them in her ears.

"Ani'Yah Nyleen Mack! I know you hear me!" my voice boomed throughout the car.

"Who the fuck do you think I is? You ain't *fuckin' with* no average bitch, boy!" she sang aloud instead of answering my call.

This broad was crazy. Her ass was sitting here changing the words to Beyoncé's song. This kiddie shit had gotten old really quick. I threw the hazard lights on and pulled over to the side of the road. I hopped out the car faster than she could comprehend. I snatched the door open and yanked an AirPod out of her ear.

"Let's get some shit straight right here and right now. When I call yo fuckin' name, answer. Most importantly, I don't do this kiddie shit. You're a grown ass woman in charge of the biggest organization in the fuckin' world. Act like you got some fuckin' sense. If you don't wanna talk about last night that's fine, but you will not ignore me. That's the easiest way to piss me off. Do you understand me, Ani?"

The area was pitch-black, and the light from the car illuminated her face. Even when she was steaming mad, Ani was a sight to see. Her gorgeous dark chocolate skin was smooth like the finest silk. I could feel her burning a hole into my face as she sat there steaming mad. She wanted to say something, yet the look on my face caused her to rethink any thoughts of getting flip at the mouth with me. Instead of opening her mouth, she held out her hand in hopes that I would return the AirPod. If she wanted to play kiddie ass games, then I was gonna play them with her. I put it in my breast pocket and slammed the door closed.

"Owen! Give me my damn AirPod!" Now she wanted to open her damn mouth. She wasn't talking that tough shit when I was in her face.

"Ani, all of this could have been avoided if you would have just answered my question." I turned the music up and got back on the expressway.

When we were on the side of the road, I noticed that there was a fleet of headlights in a perfect line about a mile behind us. Not many people used this expressway at this time of night. Shit was about to get messy real quick. The cars were going down the road quicker than I anticipated.

I turned the music down so that she could hear me. "Ani, put your seatbelt on?"

"Oh, you're talking to me again?"

"Ani, put your fuckin' seatbelt on! God, why are you so fuckin' diffi—"

I wasn't able to get the words out before a truck rammed into the back of us sending Ani flying into the front seat.

"This is why I told your hardheaded ass to put on your fuckin' seat belt!"

I didn't mean to yell at her, but this is why we were in most of our situations. She's stubborn and hardheaded. She was not the same person that I met a few weeks back. That girl was much more reserved and gentler.

"If you would have just told me that someone was following us then I would have been prepared! Where's your extra gun?"

The car rammed us again, and we had about one or two more times of that before they successfully knock us off the road. We needed to act quickly. We were about to go over a half a mile-long bridge that hovered over water.

"Under the back seat. Hurry!"

She grabbed the long gun from under the seat and rolled down the windows. This shit was happening fast.

"Get your ass in this car, Ani! It's too fuckin dark out. You can't see them, but they can see you!" Her tiny ass was about to sit on the fuckin' ledge of the window to bust the gun.

"Shut up and drive Owen, damn! I got this shit." She sat on the ledge and started letting bullets fly. Whoever was behind us was returning fire. Thankfully, this truck was bulletproof. "Got one!" she yelled as she shot out the tires of the first truck, sending it flying off the road— one down, two to go.

"Ah shit!" she yelled out, and fear traveled through my body.

"Ani, what the fuck just happened? Get yo ass back in this car!" She didn't come back in and continued to shoot at the cars. Her aim was successful enough to get rid of two of the cars, but the last one was holding up. "Ani get in here, NOW!"

She finally climbed back in the car and sat the gun on the floor. That's not what caught my attention. She was holding on to her left arm. I flicked the light on and saw the blood covering the white t-shirt.

"I'm fine, Owen. Don't worry about me. Focus on getting us out of here."

We had made it over the bridge, and there was still one car left behind us. I tried to see who was behind the wheel. These attacks weren't random. From the looks of it, this shit was all calculated. Someone wanted Ani dead by any means necessary.

The truck picked up speed and pulled alongside us. The diver wore a black ski mask as well as the passenger. I searched to see if there was something that I could use to identify whoever this was. I was coming up empty-handed until the passenger smiled while pointing a gun at me.

"Owen, watch out!" Ani screamed, but it was too late.

The road had gone from two lanes to one, and concrete barriers were directly in front of us. The truck slammed into it and sent us flying. The only thing I could think of as the car soared through the air was Ani. Tears and fear were evident on her face. I reached out to grab her and held her close before the car came crashing down.

I could hear her soft whimpers as I searched for my phone to call for help. Her head was on my chest, and all I could do was run my fingers through her hair.

"911, what's your emergency?"

"Help," was all I was able to get out before everything around me faded out.

23

NOLTON JOHNSON

I don't feel any kind of remorse for what I've been doing. Kindred reneged on our deal, so shit was only going to get worse for him and his precious ass family. I've put up with a lot of shit from him in my life, and him giving everything to his punk ass daughter was the final straw.

Her inexperienced ass thought that she was the shit just because she was moving product better and making more money. If that were me, I would be doing the shit ten times better. I just needed the chance to shine and show Kindred that I had it in me. Fuck the rules of this game. This empire was supposed to be mine, and I'm not going to stop until I get everything that's owed to me.

"Damn Nole, you been busy as fuck today. First Britton and now them. Did you have to run them off the fuckin' road?"

"Shut up nigga. We didn't do that shit. They asses weren't paying attention. That's on them. Now get us the fuck out of here so that we can junk this truck." Nato exited the expressway, and we made our way back to my neck of the woods.

"You think they dead?" Nato was down for whatever when it came to my recklessness, yet once Ani took over, his ass been more scared than a hoe in church.

"Nah, they ain't dead yet. That's my plan though. I can't just take out Ani. I gotta take out everybody."

I know the shit sounded crazy, but in order for Kindred to respect me and fear me, I had to take out everyone he loved just like his brother did me. Yeah, a nigga knew all about Kendrell killing my parents. I've known about it since the day that it happened.

My parents were killed in a drive-by shooting that was executed by Kendrell. He was beefin' with some people on the same block as us and ended up ordering a hit on them. My parents got caught in the cross-fire and were dead on arrival. Kindred may not have pulled the trigger, but he knew what happened and refused to tell me that his brother was the reason I was an orphan.

We made it to the junk car lot that we used when we needed to trash a car. I needed to make this shit quick. Once we were done here, I needed to make my way to the hospital to see the damage I had done. Hopefully, her pretty little ass would be out of commission for a while. Also, I pray that this pushes her to the edge, and she gives everything to me.

"Wait, don't you want to cool out for a minute? If you head to the hospital now, then they're going to be suspicious." Nato had a point. We hopped in my other truck and went to get some grub. All this excitement had a nigga famished.

"You don't think you took this shit too far?" Ugh, this nigga was asking way too many questions for my taste.

"Man, do you ever shut the fuck up? I did what I had to do in order to get what's rightfully mind. That prissy lil' bitch doesn't deserve this shit. This is a gentleman's game. Bitches like her and her uppity ass momma are only good for one thing— suckin' this big ass dick."

"Man, chill out on all that shit. I just asked a simple question. Would your mother be proud of you if she heard you sayin' that bitches are only good for one thing? Why you gotta go and disrespect black women like that. I'm ashamed of you right now, my nigga. I'm ashamed." This fool had the nerve to shake his head as we pulled into a fast food joint.

"You think I should get her some flowers or some shit or is that too much?"

"I ain't sure, my dude. Hey, I gotta question, what are you gonna do when her friend tells her that you're the one after her? You gotta plan for that?"

I took a bite out of my burger and thought about his question. "Shit, I'm not sure. I guess I'm gonna just go with the flow. I'm more than capable of handling myself. They don't even know that I gotta few of their people on my team that are willin' to help me with this shit."

"Nigga, you sound dumb. Ya ass is gonna get caught with ya pants down, and you're gonna be shit out of luck. Did you not see how that bit—I mean that chick was bussin' that fuckin' gun. She ain't the lil' girl that you thought she was. Bussin' a long gun in the middle of the fuckin' night takes balls man—"

"You scare, lil' nigga? If you scared, then get the fuck on. I'm gonna get what's mine by any means necessary. That lil' preschool ass bitch ain't gonna take over what's mine!" I slammed my fist on the table, and everyone in the restaurant looked at me. "Fuck y'all lookin' at! Mind your fuckin' business. We good over here!"

"Calm yo fat ass down before you stroke out in this bitch. I was just making sure that you knew what the fuck you were doing. Forget I even said shit to you."

He packed up his food and walked out to the car. The shit he was saying was making sense. I just didn't want to hear it right now. If I was going to take over this shit, I needed to move better. I could feel a war brewing, and I wasn't ready for it by far. I needed to get to the hospital before Britton's ass relayed my message.

24

MARIYAH MACK

The minute Tony called me saying that Ani and Owen had been hurt I raced to get to them. I threw on some clothes and ran out of the house with the rollers still in my hair. Ani was my whole world, and I don't know what I would do if something happened to her. I put the gas pedal to the floor and did about thirty miles above the speed limit all the way to the hospital. From what Tony was telling me, they were airlifted to Christ Hospital. Our estate wasn't too far from the hospital. It only took me twenty minutes to get there.

The car came to a screeching halt when I pulled in the parking lot. I jumped out and ran to my baby. When I crossed the emergency room doors, I immediately spotted Tony. He was sitting in the corner of the room with his head down and his arms crossed. My heart raced as I walked to him. I feared the worst at this point. Someone was hurt, and I didn't know who. I was growing to like Owen, and I would be heartbroken if he died trying to protect Ani.

"Tony," my voice cracked once I reached him. His eyes were glossed over, and I just knew he was going to tell me that Ani was gone. I fell to my knees in front of him and begged for him to tell me what happened.

"I'm sorry, Riyah. I don't mean to act like this. It's just that this one could have been it. This attack could have been the one to take her out." Hearing the words that came out of his mouth came with a little relief. It's obvious that someone didn't die. However, someone was severely injured.

"Tell me who's hurt?"

"Ani suffered a graze wound on her arm. She has a few bumps, cuts, and bruises from the crash, but other than that, she's good. A little shaken up, but good nonetheless."

"And Owen?"

"Owen suffered from a sprained wrist, a concussion, a few bruised ribs, as well as cuts and bruises. The paramedics said that when they arrived, he was holding onto her for dear life. If he hadn't grabbed hold of her, then she wouldn't be here. He saved her, Mariyah. Both of them are lucky."

To hear that Owen had saved my child's life brought tears to my eyes. I needed to thank him for all that he's done. He's been with Ani since the beginning without any complaints.

"Get in touch with Britton. She'll want to be here. What are the room numbers?" He told me their room numbers, and I made my way to get a visitor pass and down the long hallways. Before I saw Ani, I wanted to see Owen. He saved my baby's life, and I needed to thank him for that. Even though this was his job, he's like family and will be treated as such.

"Knock, knock," I announced myself. Owen was lying in bed with his eyes closed. When he heard my voice, his eyes popped open, and he shifted in the bed.

"Ms. Mack, where's Ani?" he asked just above a whisper. I grabbed him a cup of ice water and held it to his mouth for him to drink.

"From what I've been told, she's fine. I haven't been to see her yet. I wanted to check on you and thank you for saving my daughter's life. They said that if you hadn't held on to her, then things would have been much worse."

"Where is she?" He had completely ignored everything I said.

"I'm not sure yet, but as soon as I find out, I'll let you know." I didn't want to lie to him. In this moment, he needed to focus on himself and get better.

"No worries, I'll find her myself. Thanks, Ms. Mack."

Owen started getting up from the bed. Something about his fight to see her threw me off. He cared for my daughter, and it was clear as day. This wasn't just a job for him. This was love, and this was him being a protector.

"Owen, listen to me. It's obvious that you want to know what's going on with Ani, but you won't be any good to her if you don't heal. Now, I'll go check on her, and hopefully, she'll be able to come to you. Is there anyone that I can call to come check on you?" He looked me in my eyes and sadness etched his face.

"Nah thanks, Ms. Mack." He laid back in the bed, took a deep breath, and closed his eyes. His phone was on the dresser, so I grabbed it and made my way to Ani's room.

As I made my way to Ani's room, I decided to take a peek into Owen's phone. Everyone had *someone* to call, and I was going to find Owen's person. There were a bunch of missed calls from a woman by the name of Camille. I pressed her name and waited for her to answer.

"Owen! Oh my gosh, is that you? Owen baby, I've been trying to get in contact with you since last night!" The woman on the other end rambled on and on and wasn't letting me get a word in.

"Um, excuse me—"

"Who is this? Why are you calling me from Owen's phone? This better not be a woman to woman type of call."

"Sweetie, I'm going to need you to take a deep breath and listen to me. Owen was in an accident, and I was calling to let you know. He's suffered from a broken arm and a few bruised ribs but other than that, he's okay. He's currently at Christ Hospital," I continued giving her information on his status. She informed me that she was his fiancée, and she would be there shortly. Once that call was completed, I entered Ani's room.

My breath was caught in my throat when I saw that my daughter's beautiful chocolate skin had dried blood and cuts on it. She had her back towards the door, and I could hear silent sobs. This was a lot for her to take in and deal with, but I had to admit, she was handling everything a lot better than I had expected.

"Ani," I called out her name and waited for a response. When there wasn't one, I walked over to the side of the bed and took a seat in front of her. "Talk to me baby, tell me what's going on?"

"Is he gone?"

"Is who gone, Ani?"

"Owen."

"No sweetie, Owen's going to be fine. He's down the hall in his own room recovering. It won't be quick, but he's going to be just fine. Now, that we've gotten that out of the way, let's talk about you. How are you feeling?" I knew Ani a lot better than she thought I did. Her body language and her mood were telling me a story.

"How do you know when you love someone?" This question took me by surprise. I knew that she and Manny were seeing each other. However, I did not know that it was this serious.

"You think you're in love with Manny?" She quickly turned around with fire dancing in her eyes.

"Hell no! Fuck Manny, and I hope he burns in hell!" Tears streamed down her face, and I had no clue what was happening. "He's probably showing the devil his passport by now."

"Ani, do you mind telling me what's going on? What happened with Manny?" She held her head down and started to tell me everything that happened with Manny. My heart didn't know how to react. On the one hand, I was happy that my child was safe and out of his way. On the other, I'm pissed that she had to deal with this on her own. Why didn't she call me?

"I'm good, mom. I promise." I felt that there was much more to this story that she wasn't telling me, but I wasn't going to push the subject.

"Where's Owen? I want to see him." I gave her his room number and helped her out of bed. She grabbed her IV pole and started down the hallway.

When we arrived at the room, a beautiful model-like woman was standing over Owen caressing his head. His meds must have been administered because he was knocked out cold. She heard us come in the room and her head immediately shot up.

"Hi, are you the woman who called me?" I nodded, and she walked over and wrapped her arms around me.

"Thank you so much for letting me know about my fiancée. I've been worried sick about him." She took a step back and looked me up and down. "Gosh, you're gorgeous."

"I'm sorry. Did you say you were his fiancée?" Ani walked up next to me and anger etched her face.

"Yes, I'm Camille De Lina, Owen's fiancée." She walked towards Ani with her hand outstretched showing off a fat ass rock. Ani hesitated with the gesture, but eventually, she gave in and shook her hand.

"Nice to meet you. I'm Ani." Camille's face quickly dropped into a frown. Something tells me that this was going to get ugly.

I don't know what the fuck was going on between these three, but that wasn't my main concern. My main concern was the fact that this woman stated that her last name was Del Lina. The same Del Lina crew that wanted to take over Kindred's territory. For the past few years, they've kept things civil. However, I could feel it in my gut that things were about to take a turn for the worst. Two of the biggest cartel families stood in this hospital room, and neither of them knew otherwise.

"Would you please excuse us for a moment? Ani, may I have a word with you outside?" By this time, Owen's eyes were opening up, and when he saw Ani, it's as if his eyes brightened.

"Oh, Owen baby, you're awake!" Camille placed her face in front of his and repeatedly kissed his lips. His face frowned just as Ani turned her back to him. This was about to be a hot mess. There wasn't enough wine in the world to prepare me for the storms that were about to take place.

"Ani, I need you to tell me what's going on? And it needs to happen quickly before she finds out who you *really* are."

"What are you talkin' about, ma?"

She could sit here and play dumb with me all she wanted, but I knew better. She and Owen had something going on, and the shit was going to hit the fan if lil' mama back there found out Ani's secrets.

The Del Lina family has been after the Edwards territory since the very beginning. The Edwards Cartel owned about seventy-five percent of the nation's finest cocaine. The other twenty-five percent belonged to the Del Lina's. After years of battling, a peace treaty was formed. The De Lina Cartel was able to control the West Coast from California to Mexico. According to the deal, their product was to never cross over into Edwards' territory. If it did, then we'd have a war on our hands.

"Ani, do you know who that woman is?" She shook her head no. Now I know Ani read everything there was to know about this damn organization and yet, she couldn't remember who the Del Lina's were.

Before we could get into that conversation, Owen called out for her.

"Ani, don't walk yo ass back into that room while his fiancée is still in there. That's going to open up a can of worms that we're not ready for in any capacity."

Of course, against my warning, Ani rolled her eyes and walked back into that main room.

25

ANI MACK

There wasn't a bitch on this earth that I was afraid of at this point, except for my mama. I've damn near died on multiple occasions by a coward that won't show themselves, and I'll be damned if a bitch is going to run me away from my... Wait, I need to get a hold of myself. This woman clearly just stated that she's Owen's fiancée, and I had bigger shit to deal with.

Instead of going into the room on some tough shit, I decided to switch it up. My mother was warning me about this woman for a reason, and as soon as I was discharged from this hospital, I was going to find out everything that I needed to know about her.

When I walked into the room, it looked as if they were having a heated discussion. "I can come back later," I said while turning towards the door.

"No!" Owen sat up in the bed with a mug on his face.

"Nah, it's obvious that y'all have some pre-marital issues to work out. I'll come check on you before I'm discharged. I'll also speak to the doctors about your recovery times and when we can expect you to come back to work. Take care, Owen. I'll have Tony get you anything you need."

I started walking out of the room thinking that everything would be all good. That is until a hand touched my arm and swung me around. My tattered body was in no shape to fight. However, if I needed to, I wasn't going to back down.

"I'm sorry, I don't believe that we've been properly introduced. Can you tell me how you know my fiancée?"

"Ani, you don't have to answer that," Owen said while struggling to sit up in the bed. "How are you feeling?"

"Owen, Ani and I are having a conversation sweetie. No need to intervene if there's nothing to hide." She turned her attention back to me, and I sized her up. Her manicured hand was still attached to my arm. I snatched my arm away and took a few steps back.

"Not that I owe you an explanation...Owen is a part of my security team. Now if you'll excuse me, I need to get back to my room. You all have a great day, and again, Owen, call if you need anything. Contact Tony when you're back to your full strength." With those words, I walked out and back to my room.

I just wanted to throw these past two days away. From everything that happened with Manny, the shit that happened with Owen, and let's not forget almost losing my life. Also, I was slowly losing my mind because I could feel myself falling for Owen by the second. Seeing him with his fiancée wasn't something that I was prepared for. My head just hurts thinking about everything. I passed my mom in the hallway on the phone, and I didn't even bother stopping to talk to her. The only thing on my mind right now was getting discharged and getting some rest. My headache was growing by the minute.

As soon as my head hit the pillow, I was drifting off to sleep. That was short-lived when I heard Britton's loud ass mouth from down the hallway. I threw the pillow over my head and prayed that she came in quieter than she just was. Again, that was short-lived when she came into my room, flipped the light on, and immediately started yelling. For it to be the middle of the night, she was dressed as if she had just come from the gym. She wore a black cropped top long sleeved compression shirt, with burgundy leggings, and Nike Vapormax to match.

"Ani Nyleen Mack! Bitch, you better wake the fuck up and tell me what the fuck is going on? I've been blowing ya fuckin'—"

"Damn Britt, give her a second to answer your question." DJ came in behind her, walked over to hug me, and placed some flowers on the table next to me. "Sup, Boss Lady."

"Nah, back up DJ, if she doesn't get to talking then I'm gonna make her time here a little longer!" With my thumbs, I massaged my temples. Her mouth was real reckless right now, and it was only going to get worse when I told her everything that happened.

"DJ, do you—" before I could finish the sentence, he held his hands up, said he'd be down in the café and exited the room while closing the door behind him.

Instead of Britton taking a seat in the chair adjacent from me, she kicked off her shoes, climbed her ass in the bed, and got under the covers.

"What's been going on Ani? I need to know everything." I took a deep breath and ran down the past forty-eight hours of my life.

"Oh Ani, I'm so sorry. Why didn't you call me? I would have come helped you!" Tears were streaming down her pain-etched face. I know that I should have called her myself to let her know everything. She was the only friend that I had, and I knew she would be ten toes down for me. She was absolutely right, I should have called.

"I hate to make your night worse, but there's something that I need to tell you. I know who's after—"

"Hey, Ani bear," Nolton came busting in the room with a huge teddy bear and flowers.

"Hey Unc, what's good?" He came over to hug me and then took a seat in the chair next to my bed.

"Shit, you know, same shit different day. How you holdin' up?"

We continued with the small talk while Britton was unusually quiet. Her vibe was off, and I couldn't wait for him to leave so that she could tell me what was wrong. I'm almost positive that it had something to with her and DJ. I hope she didn't think that I didn't notice that they came in together. There was a story for her to tell me.

"Hey Britton, let's go outside and chat for a minute. I have some important information about that gym space you inquired about." Nolton looked at Britton, and I had no clue that she was looking for another space. Her current gym was a decent size. I guess she wanted more.

"Ani, I'll be right back." Her voice was shaky and dry. This wasn't something that I was used to when it came to Britton. Something was off, and she needed to tell me now.

❧ 26 ❧

BRITTON MATTHEWS

I wasn't trying to give myself away when Nolton came into the hospital room. It's just that less than a few hours ago, he was holding a knife to my neck and threatening my life. How was I supposed to react to seeing his face? My body trembled with each step that I took. When I stepped out of the door, Nolton was standing there with his arms folded.

"You told your friend yet?" I found myself pulling on the sleeves of my shirt and shaking my head. "Good, don't tell her shit. If you try to save her, then I'm comin' to kill you and ya whole family tree. You understand me. If you even think about warning her Britton then so help me God, I'm going to make your life a living hell. Do you understand?"

Tears welled in the brim of my eyes. He was standing here threatening the life of someone that came to my rescue when I first moved to Chicago. I loved Ani like she was my own sister. In our short amount of time together, we'd been through so much. She knew every single detail about my life and didn't judge me once. How was I supposed to sit here and let this happen? I was stuck at an impasse.

"I'll be checkin' in with you, Britton. Give Ani my best." He walked off, and I wanted to break down and cry. How the hell did I get stuck in this position?

I couldn't return to her room without getting myself together first. If she even hinted that something was wrong with me, she was going to dig until I gave in. Something needed to be done before it was too late, and I was burying my best friend.

"Everything okay, Britton?" My soul left my body when Ms. Mack put her hand on my shoulder. "Why are you so jumpy? Tell me what's going on?"

I turned to look at her, and I lost it. I wasn't going to sit here and not tell someone everything that I knew. Nolton was dumber than a box of rocks if he thought that I was going to sit here and listen to his ass. If he were so smart, then he would know that the only family that I had was in this hospital.

"I can't tell you right now, but we need to get Ani moved out of here as soon as possible. I know who's after her." Her eyes grew wide as she pulled out her phone. She pressed a few buttons and then held it to her ear.

"Tony, we gotta move." She finished talking to him and then placed the phone back in her purse. "Have you said anything to Ani?"

"No, ma'am."

"Good, keep it that way. She's been through more than enough these past two days. I'm afraid that if we add anything else to her plate, she's going to end up in the insane asylum. Dammit, I didn't bring her any clothes."

"I got her, mama." I placed a hand on her shoulder, and she took a deep breath. Ever since Ani got into this game, it's been nothing short of madness. Something needed to give. My friend needed to see some kind of sunshine soon.

DJ came running with the clothes, he had some business that he needed to handle but assured me that he would get up with me tomorrow. We kissed each other goodbye, and then mama and I got Ani dressed and out of that hospital. The doctors wanted her to stay overnight for observation, but we weren't letting that happen. She was too defenseless in such an open space. If she needed further care, then we would hire someone to come out to the estate.

During the ride, not a sound was made throughout the car. Everyone was deep into their own thoughts. The air was thick, and there were so many questions that needed to be answered. Mama Mack mentioned that she's been through a lot these past few days, and I wanted to know exactly what happened. Right now, I just needed a hot shower and a good night's sleep. The cars pulled into the gate, and we all retreated into the house. Tony and Ziggy got Ani settled into her room while I went to mine. I appreciated the fact that I had something set up out here.

As I stood in the shower, all of today's events swarmed through my head. Tears welled in my eyes once again, but this time there was no stopping them. Everything that I had been holding in since this morning came pouring out and mixing with the water. The cut on my neck started to sting. I had completely forgotten that it was even there. It only caused me to cry out even harder. I tried to stop them, but they kept coming.

"Britton? Britton sweetie, what's wrong?"

Mama Mack came busting in the bathroom to check on me. She didn't give a damn that I was as naked as the day I was born. Her only focus was comforting me and seeing what was wrong. She stepped in with all her clothes on and held me. Just when I thought I was crying the hardest I'd ever been, a scream escaped from the depths of my soul.

"Baby, I can't help you if you don't tell me what's wrong? I need to know everything that's going on, Britton. Lord, help us all. There's far too much going on right now. Wrap your loving arms around this whole family."

She prayed over me and then cut the water in the shower off. Her motherly compassion towards me was something that I longed for. She grabbed a towel off the warmer and wrapped it around me. I threw my head back to stop the tears, and that's when she saw the stitches on my neck.

"Britton, what's going on how did this happen? "

"I-I know who's after Ani. He told me that if I say anything, then he'll kill my whole family. You guys are the only family that I know, and

I don't want anything to happen to you!" My sobs grew louder and louder as she rubbed my back.

"Britton, there's not a soul on this earth that I am afraid of. Tell me who's after my family." She tilted my head up so that we were eye to eye.

"Nolton." His name rolled off my tongue, and a wave of relief rushed over me. Mariyah's eye's turned cold. I've never seen this look on her face.

"Why is he trying to kill me?" Ani came in the bathroom with a scowl on her face. All I could do was sit there baffled. I'm almost positive that this isn't how we wanted her to find out. Honestly, I didn't want her to find out about it at all.

"I'm not sure sweetie, but I know who might be able to tell you."

27

KINDRED EDWARDS

"Edwards, you have a visitor!" the guard whispered, waking me up.

My schedule didn't consist of any visitors today, and it damn sure wasn't visitin' hours. It was the crack of dawn. If I had to guess, it was about five in the fuckin' morning.

"Come on. You don't have much time."

Since I've been in here, I've gotten along with most of the guards. Once they found out who I was, they flocked to me like flies to shit. No one wanted to be on my bad side, and I appreciated that shit. My accommodations quickly improved. These niggas went out of their way to make my bid easier. The night guard came into my cell, cuffed me, and escorted me into a room that I've never seen before.

"Wait here."

He left out of the room and came back a few minutes later. The door opened and in walked the female version of me, and my heart damn near fell out of my chest. She was more beautiful than when I saw her at the courthouse. I'd waited time and time again for this moment and it was finally happening. Seeing my daughter up close and personal was something that I would never forget. The pictures that

Tony sent didn't do her justice. Mariyah and I did good. We created the most gorgeous woman in the world, and I wasn't just saying that because I was her father.

"Ani." She held up her hand to stop me from talking.

This must have been the attitude that Tony and Mariyah were talking about. I understood her frustrations with me, and they were all justified. However, no child of mine was going to disrespect me.

She took a seat in the chair across from me and sized me up like I was a lil' nigga on the street. She had me fucked up to the tenth power, and I see that I'm gonna have to break my foot off in her.

"We have some shit to discuss," she said with her arms folded.

"Before we can move forward in conversation, you need to understand that I don't tolerate disrespect, Ani'Yah."

"And I don't tolerate deadbeat fathers. Now that we've established what we don't tolerate let's get to the reason why I'm here. Kindred, right now I'm not in the business of building a relationship with you. Right now, I'm focused on trying to live to see another day. At this moment, Nolton Johnson is doing everything in his power to take me out. Some kinda right hand man you have," she mumbled under her breath. "Look, all that I ask of you right now is to tell me why he's hell-bent on ending my life."

She sat back in the chair with her arms folded and a mean mug graced her face. This girl was more like her mother than I thought. I was going to have to change my approach with her real quick. Talkin' nice to Ani wasn't going to cut it. She wanted to get gutta with me then so fuckin' be it.

"Little girl, I don't know who the fuck you think you're talking to, but it ain't me. Don't let this orange ass suit fool you. I have no problem forgetting that you came from my nut sack."

Her eyes formed into slits and her chest heaved up and down.

"Now I'm going to answer your question, but the next time you call yourself gettin' disrespectful, we're gonna have a whole fuckin' problem. Now, Nolton believed that if anything happened to me that he was entitled everything, but he was sadly mistaken. I knew that you were out there, and I was banking on you stepping up to the plate. I'm actually glad that you did.

Nolton has been my right hand since we were young. His parents died at the hands of my brother, Kendrell. Ever since then, I've had him under my wing and grooming him to be just like us. Once his parents were gone, he lived, ate, shit, and breathed the cartel life. I shouldn't have felt guilty for my brother's actions, but I did, and I created a money hungry nigga in the process. I had my suspicions about him and you coming in here only confirms them. He's going to try everything in his power to take over the business. I can't do much to help you from in here. However, a word of advice, a pretty bitch is any mans weakness."

"Cool. Find a bitch that's gonna make him weak in the knees and take him out that way, got it." She stood up to leave, and I grabbed her arm.

"Hey, nothing that I say or do is going to make up the twenty-two years that I missed out on. And I say twenty-two because I was there for the first two years. You were too young to remember and Riyah burned any trace of it. Just know that I was there, and I always loved you. Ani, I'll never stop loving you. I was there every step of the way, just not how I should have been, and for that, I apologize. I hope that you'll allow me into your heart and give me a chance to be a father to you. I'll always love you, Ani." I rolled up my sleeve and showed her the tattoo that I had with her and Mariyah's names. They were the loves of my life, and I'll do whatever it takes to make this shit right.

A puddle of water formed under her eyes as she looked at the tattoo. "Maybe...maybe I'll come visit you again. But for now, I need to focus on the task at hand." She wiped her face with the back of her hand and straightened herself out. "I'll let you know how everything works out." She tapped on the door for the guard to open. Before she walked out, she turned around to look at me and then ran over to hug me.

"Don't think all is forgiven. It's going to take a lot more than a tattoo and an apology for me to forgive you. I may be tough out here in the drug world, but at the end of the day, I'm still a girl who always wanted her father around. Make it right with my mother, and then we can work on us."

She disappeared out into the darkness of the hallways, and my heart was full. A nigga like me doesn't get choked up much, but hearing that she was willing to give me another chance had to be one of the best feelings in the world. I prayed to the heavens above to cover her and let her come out of this alive.

❧ 28 ❧

ANI MACK

Going to see Kindred gave me plenty of mixed emotions. On the one hand, I was thankful that he had the information that I needed to get to Nolton before he got to me. Then, on the other hand, I was a sad little girl who missed having a father in her life. He needed to be there for me to answer all the questions that I had about life, boys, etc. Maybe he would have been able to see that Manny was a fuck boy and that Owen was no good for me.

As much as I wanted to dwell on that, I couldn't. I had to figure out a plan to get to Nolton. By the time I made it back to the estate, the sun was up. Tony was going to have a fuckin' fit when he found out that I took a car to go see Kindred. My safety was compromised, but it was needed.

When I pulled into the gates, everything was still calm. I parked the car the same way I found it and retreated into the house as quietly as I could. Sleep was knocking at my door, and my body was still sore from the accident. However, there was no time for that.

"Ani'Yah Nyleen Mack."

Why did people feel the need to use my whole government name when they wanted my attention? I turned to face Tony who was sitting on the steps with his arms folded like he was disappointed in my actions.

"Mornin' Tony, um, it's been a long night, and the doctor ordered that I get plenty of rest. If you don't mind, I'm gonna go ahead and do that." I turned around to walk up the other flight of stairs.

"How's Big Kin doing? Did you get the answers you were looking for? Wait, how did you get into the jail? These ain't visiting hours?"

How did he know I went to see him?

"I have my ways. Next time you decide to leave at the crack of dawn, don't take the car that I drive on a daily. I get alerts to my phone when it's been unlocked and started."

Damn, I needed to make better choices.

"It pays to be Kindred's daughter. And yes, I got the answers I needed."

"You gonna tell me who's after you?"

I wanted to tell him, but this was something that I needed to handle on my own. If I told him, then he was going to figure out a way to do it so that I didn't have to lift a finger. However, I'm not a pampered princess. The only way that people were going to respect me is if I got my hands dirty. Just because I'm a woman doesn't mean that I couldn't emotionally detach myself from this.

"Nah, it's gonna be handled. I need to ask you a favor though. When the time comes, I'm going to need you to look the other way. Things are going to get a little messy."

I didn't want to go into detail with Tony. It's not that I didn't trust him. It's just that this needed to be done under the radar.

"Ani, I have faith in whatever you got planned. Be careful. Your parents will never forgive me if I ever let something happen to you."

I nodded and retreated to my room. If things were going to work in my favor, I was only going to have a few hours of sleep before I had to start planning.

Before I could even fall in the bed, there was a knock at my door. The day hadn't even officially started, and people were already knocking. Maybe if I pretended to be sleep, they would go away. Quickly and quietly, I climbed in the bed and hid under the covers. The only thing on my mind right now was sleeping and executing this plan. Nothing else mattered to me right now.

"Ani." Owen's voice filled the room and caused my heart to swell. "Can I come in?"

"You've already opened the door."

Even though my heart was yearning for him, we couldn't be together, not by a long shot. He was an engaged man and failed to mention that piece of information. After the night before, I was positive that I wanted nothing more than to be with him. It's like we clicked instantly, and it's as if our hearts belonged together. I don't know how all of this happened. It just...happened.

"You got a minute to talk?"

Hell no, I don't want to talk to you! My mind was saying one thing, yet my mouth decided to say otherwise.

"Make it quick. I'm tryna get some sleep." The door to my room closed and the other side of the bed sank in. "Why aren't you in the hospital?"

"They aren't my thing, especially not after my pops just died."

I had forgotten all about that. Too many things have happened in such a short period of time that it was hard for me to keep up. One of these days, my head was going to explode.

"What do you need to talk about?"

He took a deep breath and let it out slowly. "I wanted to tell you about Camille. It's just that—"

"Nope stop right there. You will not sit next to me and make up an excuse for what happened. I don't regret what happened between us Owen. I just wish I would have known all the facts. We made a mistake, but trust and believe it won't happen again." At this point, I was frustrated. "And I suggest you find out who you're laying down with." He raised his eyebrow at me to try and see what I was referring to.

"You done?" I flipped the cover off of me and turned towards him with a face full of rage. "Calm ya hot ass down. Now I've let you say more than enough, but you're going to listen to me and listen to me well. Camille and I aren't even fuckin' engaged. You know how much money I make, Ani. I can't afford a fuckin' ring like that!" His voice boomed throughout the room, causing me to feel small.

"I-I didn't know."

"Of course, you didn't know. You never allowed me to tell you! Ani, I-I don't love her alright? I never have, and I never will. I ain't one to bad mouth a bitch, especially one that's been there for me after everything that I've gone through. She's been there for me and…and I felt obligated to stay. Lately, I feel as if I've just been existing when I'm around her. Yet, when I'm around you, I feel like I have a purpose. I just need you to know that you don't know everything about me, but in due time we'll have that talk. I'm sorry that this shit doesn't make sense. I don't even know what I'm trying to say. Just know that she's not the one that I want." He hung his head and swiped his free hand down his face.

The sun was now shining brightly through the blinds, allowing me to see the stress displayed on his face. We were equally fucked up in the head and had no clue where to go from here. Instead of having a conversation about everything he just said, he started on something completely different.

"Mariyah told me to take few weeks off to heal. Reggie is my replacement for now, and he'll be with you until I get back. I'll see you at the funeral. Take care, Ani." He kissed my forehead and walked out of the room leaving me speechless. At this point, my head was spinning, and it wasn't going to allow me to get the sleep that I needed.

I laid back in the bed and stared at the ceiling. Instead of getting sleep, I had to figure out a way to get to Nolton and end this before it ended me. Kindred's words rang in my ears, and I had figured out the perfect plan. It was going to take some major convincing, but I'm almost positive that I will be able to pull it off.

Once I got Nolton out of the way, then I could focus on figuring out who Owen's woman was. My mother let me know that she was someone of importance and told me to hold off on that. Digging right now wouldn't be in my best interest. I would only be adding much more on my plate.

❧ 29 ❧

OWEN PIERCE

Against doctors' advice, I checked myself out of the hospital. I ended up telling them to give me some pain meds and send me on my way. The only thing on my mind was Ani. I needed to check on her and explain everything before she started makin' up shit in her head. We'd been through too much these past couple of nights, and I felt that I owed her the truth.

Before I could put my key in the door, I could hear Camille running to open the door. She flung it open and damn near snatched me with it. Heat radiated off her body, and I just knew that I wasn't about to get any sleep. Her eyes were bloodshot red, and her tan face was puffy and red. She'd been crying her life away.

"Who is she, Owen?! Who is Ani, and why is she pretending that you work for her? How long have you been sleeping with her?" She ran up on me and started pointing her finger in my face. The pounding in my head grew louder, and if she knew what was good for her, then she's turn around and get the fuck out of my face.

"I'm not doing this shit with you," I push past her and slammed the door behind me. "I'm going to shower and go to bed."

"No, we're going to do this today. You come in here smelling like her and expect me to believe that you don't have anything going on!"

"I smell like her because I held onto her in order to save her fuckin' life, and I ain't took a shower yet! Damn, are you really that insecure that you can't take this for what it is?"

"You will not throw this back on me, Owen. I've done nothing but be there for you. In the past few months, you've changed. You've become so short with me, and I don't know what I've done. I've been there for you when you had nothing! I took care of you and never asked for anything in return, and this is how you repay me?"

This is why I refused to let her or her father help me in any way. Niggas always throw shit in your face when things aren't going their way.

"YOU AIN'T DID SHIT FOR ME THAT I HAVEN'T DONE FOR MY FUCKIN' SELF! Get the fuck out my way."

At this point, if I stayed here any longer, I'd end up knocking her head through a wall. One thing about me, I've always had a badass temper, and I didn't have time to catch a case. I needed to get away from her. I went to the closet and started throwing shit in a duffle bag.

"Wait where do you think you're going? You will not go be with her!" She came up to me and started snatching my things out of the bag.

"Man, move out my way."

There was only so much fighting that I could do. The pain meds were wearing off, and my body was going to shut down soon. I needed to get my ass out of here and away from her. Fuck it. I'll just grab some clothes in the morning. Times like this made me want to kick my ass for not having a backup pair of clothes in my car. I grabbed my keys off of the side table and walked to the door.

"Owen, please don't go. I'm so sorry!"

Tears streamed down her face, the same beautiful face that I had called myself falling in love with. We did this shit so much that I had become numb to it. Actually, I've become numb to it all. This shit never ended with her. She was going to cry, whine, and even try to have sex in order to get me to stay. That may have worked before, but not this time.

"Please, let me make it up to you. You won't be able to work for a few weeks due to the injuries. Let's take a trip to somewhere tropical and get back on track. Owen, I love you, and the only thing that I want out of life is to make this work. Please just let me try."

"Give me a day to think about everything. Also, I can't leave town. The funeral is in a few days. For right now I need space." Her face twisted and before she could even fix her mouth to say anything, I let her know what it was. "Alone, I'm not going to see Ani or anybody else. I just want to be by myself right now. I need time to process everything, Mil."

This time, she allowed me to pack my bag and leave out of the apartment without a fight.

❦ 30 ❦

BRITTON

For the past few days, Ani's been wallowing around with her head in the clouds. There's been so much going on lately and honestly, and I'm afraid that it's going to break her. I know that she's been putting on a brave face for everyone. However, I know her better than them. She's been harboring her feelings and eventually, she's going to snap. I just pray for the poor soul that will feel her wrath.

"Ani, are you ready?"

Today was the day of Owen's father's funeral. It was a hard day for all of us. We hadn't had the pleasure to meet Mr. Pierce, but Owen was a part of this family now, so we were going to be there for him.

"Yeah, let me just put on my shoes."

I can honestly say that Ani's wardrobe had come around full circle. She was going to this funeral looking nothing less than perfect. Her body looked amazing in the long-sleeved black tube dress. She paired it with five-inch black booties and a beige wrap around coat. The girl looked damn good. She almost made me go change.

"You look fine, Britt. It's a funeral, not a fashion show." She was right, but still, I couldn't be out here lacking.

A knock on the door caught out attention. "Ladies, the car is ready whenever you are." Reggie, Owen's replacement, smiled at us and then closed the door behind him.

"We'll be down in a minute, damn!" Ani rolled her eyes and got up to put on her coat.

That poor boy didn't stand a chance. Hopefully, these next couple of weeks fly past. She'd been giving him absolute hell these past few days, and I don't know how much longer he was going to last.

"Chill Ani. He's just doing his job. I know he's not Owen, but let the poor boy do what he's been trained to do." She plopped down on the bed and held her head down.

"I know. I'll apologize to him. I just hate the way that I'm feeling right now."

"You miss him, don't you?"

"Is it that obvious?"

Hell yeah, it's that obvious. She's been walking around here with the biggest attitude and firing off order after order. If she hadn't realized it by the end of the day, I was most definitely going to tell her about herself. Trust and believe. I understand what it feels like to let go of the man that your heart craves. DJ had a dangerous hold on me. When I left Philly, there wasn't a day that went by where I wasn't mad at the world and cursing someone out. That's when Mama Mack came to rescue me from self-destruction.

"It's obvious to me because I know you. This isn't you, Ani. Trust and believe that I love the woman you've blossomed into. However, you need to know when to turn it on and off. You gotta chill out, mama. It's going to be okay. Let's go before we're late."

She didn't say anything after that. She just got up and followed me out of the house. Reggie was standing by the car with the door opened. Before Ani got in the car, she whispered something in his ear that caused a smile to form on his face. If she didn't say it aloud, then it wasn't my business to know. I'm just happy that we're on the right track. We got in the car and made our way to the church.

When we made it, there were tons of people there for Mr. Pierce. It's obvious that he was loved and well respected. This may have been a nice thing for most people. However, this put Ani in a vulnerable position. Reggie opened the door, and I got out first.

It was now my turn to whisper in his ear, "Make sure you're alert and strapped." Even though this was a funeral, anything could happen. He nodded in agreement and flashed me his piece.

We entered the doors of the church and went to greet Owen and his family. By now, Ani had put on a pair of oversized sunglasses to hide her true feelings. I knew that this was going to be hard for her for more than one reason. She was fighting how she felt for him, and it was completely understandable. Her heart was pulling her towards him, but he was already accounted for, and she couldn't do anything about it.

I opted to greet Owen first to give Ani time to collect herself. I didn't even notice that his fiancée was sitting next to him.

"Hey Owen, I'm so sorry for your lost. You're in my thoughts and prayers. If there's anything you need, please feel free to let me know."

"Thanks, Britt, I appreciate that." Owen hugged me. I stepped to the side so that Ani could greet him.

"Ani, thank you for putting everything together. All of this wouldn't be possible without you." Owen touched her elbow, and if you were paying attention like I was, you would be able to see the spark between them. Owen gazed into her eyes and told her a story without saying a word. This story consisted of lust and love. Something happened between these two, and I needed to be looped in. For now, I had to stop this blatant disrespect. Sooner or later, Camille was going to catch on. I had no plans of fighting in six-inch heels today.

"We're going to go take our seats now. We'll catch up later."

They snapped out of their trance at the same time, and embarrassment flushed their faces. I couldn't wait to find out what the hell happened between the two of them. This shit was much deeper than I thought.

The service started, and it was absolutely beautiful, and many tears were shed. Ani had really done a good job at coordinating everything. The kind words that were shared about him made me I wish we had been able to meet.

"Ani, darling, may I have a moment of your time?"

We were standing on the steps of the church waiting for Reggie to bring the car around. Our next destination was to go to the cemetery for the burial. We both turned around and came face to face with Camille.

"No, thank you."

Ani began walking down the steps completely ignoring Camille's question. Before Ani could get to the end of the stairs, Camille grabbed her elbow. The shit happened so fast that I wasn't able to stop the fire that was burning slow in Ani.

"Touch me again, and I'll chop your fuckin' hand off," Ani spoke low through gritted teeth. Most people would be terrified when someone threatened to chop their hand off, but Camille wasn't fazed. Something was off about her, and I needed to find out.

"Oh Ani, why are you so hostile with me? I just wanted to thank you for taking the time out to organize all of this. It was truly a lovely service. Owen and I appreciate all that you've done." She released her hand off Ani's elbow and then leaned over to whisper in her ear, "Anything you can do, I can do better. Your threats don't scare me."

Ani was getting ready to lunge at Camille, but Reggie came and held her back. This shit was getting uglier by the minute. We had enough on our plates and didn't need to add petty, unnecessary drama. He led her to the car, and I climbed in right behind her.

"Ani! What the hell is going on? Please tell me what the fuck is going on? This ain't you by far. Get to spilling the tea!" I snapped my fingers at her to get her talking.

"Now's not the time, Britt," she warned me.

"No, it is time. You've been walking around here this past week like hell on wheels. I understand that you've been through a lot but I need you to not let that be the end all be all.

During our time at the cemetery, things remained calm and cool. Owen stole glances at Ani every chance he got. Camille could act like she didn't see it, but I know she did. I needed to figure out who she was before this blows up into something bigger.

❧ 31 ❧

ANI MACK

Now that the funeral was done, it was time for me to get things moving with Nolton. He's been rather quiet lately. I guess it's due to the new woman in his life. He'd been engulfed in his new relationship, and I couldn't blame him. He had a nice ass woman on his arm. She had the body of a goddess, the smile of an angel, but a heart as cold as ice. She was a black widow type of woman.

"How's our girl doing?" I asked Britton as she walked into the house.

"She's going good. She's got that nigga wrapped around her fingers. Paisley was definitely the best choice for this. Lil mama is quick and deadly. It's only been a few days, and he damn near about to marry her ass. She hasn't even let him sniff the cookies." We both erupted in laughter.

After much convincing, a non-disclosure agreement, and a few Chanel bags later, we were able to get Paisley on board for our plan. She didn't know why she was doing what she was doing, but she was down for whatever. Like Nicki Minaj said, "them Chanel bags is a bad habit."

"What's their next move?" I asked as we sat on the front steps of the estate.

We had plenty of places that we could lounge around in this mansion. However, nothing felt better than sitting outside, on the steps, in the summer sun enjoying slushies and flaming hots with meat and cheese. I live for simple moments like this. No matter where I go in life, I'll always be the little black girl from the south side of Chicago.

"Slow down killa, don't choke on those chips. Why are you even eating that garbage?"

"Chalk it up to stress. I'll get back to eating right once this is handled."

"Are you stressing over Nolton or Owen? I heard he went out of town for a few days." Britton placed her straw in her mouth and gave me a "knowing" look.

"I'm not stressing over Owen," I lied. Of course, I was stressing over him. I hadn't seen him since the funeral. When Brit said that he was out of town, my mind instantly went to him being with *her*. Never in my life have I been the jealous type. Yet, here I am stressing over Owen Pierce.

"Just admit it, Ani. You have feelings for him. I want to be the first to tell you that it's okay. He's a good-looking guy, hard worker, and trying to make an honest living. Shit, if I were you, I'd be all over that — every day, every second of the day. Admit you have feelings for him. It will make you feel better."

"Who does she have feelings for?"

We both turned around and saw my mom leaning against the two double doors. I didn't even hear her come up. My mouth fell open when I saw what she was wearing. She had on a body-hugging sleeveless dress that stopped right under her knees and a pair of open toe wedges. Her hair was freshly done in a blowout, and her makeup was done to perfection.

"Forget who she likes for just a second...Damn, Mama Mack! Who knew you were hiding all that back there! Turn around and let me see you!"

Britton jumped up, walked over to her, and twirled her around. It was no secret that my mama was carrying a wagon back there, no secret at all. She just hid it well with her clothes.

"Where are you going with that tight ass dress on? And does Kindred know this?"

"First of all, I'm grown Ani, and no he does not because we are not together. Kindred is *your* father, not *mine*. Therefore, I can wear what I want when I want. Understood?" she sassed with her hands on her hips.

"Understood. I also understand that he's probably pissed you off, and now you're out here about to bring some man into the line of fire to die. Do you boo! Do you...but make sure that man you're going to see can shoot!"

I fell over and laughed until tears fell from my eyes. My mama could play all day if she wanted, but what she won't do is sit here and act like she doesn't love Kindred. I've heard the late-night conversations, and I know that she's been visiting him more than usual.

"Anyway, enough about me and what I'm wearing, answer my question. Who's got you in your feelings?" She folded her arms across her chest and waited for an answer.

"Nobody," I stated with a straight face. She wasn't about to lecture the hell out of me. She's already warned me once about Owen and his fiancée. I refused to hear it again.

"Owen," Britton coughed out, and I could have killed her. She had better be lucky that I didn't have my gun near me.

"Oh really?"

Before she could dig in me, her cell went off. She spoke for a few minutes and then rolled her eyes before hanging up the call.

"This conversation isn't over, Ani'Yah. I gotta go, you girls be good tonight. Don't get into any trouble."

She went inside, grabbed her purse, and came right back out. The gates to the estate opened, and a black Mercedes Benz rolled up. The driver never exited the vehicle. Strike one. Whoever this man is didn't even have the decency to come and open the door for her.

"Ani, chill! I can see the smoke coming out of your ears! I'll see you ladies later." She quickly opened the door and slid right in.

"Damn, I'm tryna be like yo mama when I get older." Britton

thought this shit was hilarious. I'm all for my mama dating and moving on with her life, but deep down, I still held an ounce of hope that they would get it together.

The sun was starting to set indicating that we had been out here for a good part of the day. This was just what I needed, time with my best friend, living a normal life. There aren't too many days like this in my life anymore, and I appreciated the days that I could do this. Britton's phone started ringing and caused me to snap back to reality.

"Hey, Paisley, what's good?" She placed the phone on speaker so that I could hear what was going on.

"Everything is a go for tonight. I'll text you when it's all set to go." That was all the confirmation that I needed. Both of us jumped off the steps and ran into the house. The time was now or never.

We had everything we needed already set to the side. Britton and I grabbed everything we needed and ran towards the door. When we reached the door, Tony was standing in front of it with his arms folded. I didn't have time for his shit, we needed a truck, and we needed it quick. I went to open my mouth, but he held his hand up in protest.

"Here," he tossed something my way, and I caught it. It was a set of car keys. "Do what you have to do but be safe. Your father will kill me if anything happens to you. Are you sure that you don't want the extra back up? He's tried on multiple attempts to kill you and has almost been successful. You are sure you got this?"

"Yeah, I'll be good. I promise." I hugged him, and we ran to the truck.

"It's bulletproof, Ani! Remember that!" he yelled after us as I sped out of the gates.

Ever since that morning that I visited Kindred, I had been working on figuring out how I was going to catch Nolton. I'd been watching his every move for a week, and that's when I figured it out. Paisley was the perfect person to reel him in. She was young, gorgeous, and thicker than day-old grits.

Nolton loved hanging out at this old pool hall out in the south burbs. He visited it every single night at the same time. Paisley was able to sink her hooks into him the first night. As soon as he saw her, his mouth salivated, and he wanted everything she had to offer.

That's sloppy work if you ask me. What's even funnier is the fact that every employee inside there was loyal to the Edwards family. If I'd been out here threatening the life of the heir to one of the biggest cartels in the nation, I'd be a little more aware of my surroundings and switching up my schedule if I were him. He's walking around as if he's untouchable. That ends tonight.

❧ 32 ❧

NOLTON JOHNSON

"**B**aby girl, don't start no shit you can't finish. You're going up against a man that's been doing this shit since before you were born."

Lately, I've been laying low on taking out Ani. I fucked up and brought too much attention to myself. Once word got out to Kindred, I'd end up running for my life. I've been doing a lot of thinking...I don't want this life anymore. It was fun while it lasted. The new woman in my life was spittin' some real shit to me, basically letting me know that there was a whole world out there for me to explore.

"Ha! I finish everything I start, baby." She seductively licked her lips. Tonight, was the night that I was gonna break her ass in. She's been holding out on a nigga these past few weeks, but that ended tonight.

"Aight lil mama, rack 'em up."

We'd been here at the pool hall that Kindred and I frequented since we were shorties. There weren't many of these left in this day and age. That's why I was here damn near every day. Keepin' them in business was my main goal.

"Shoot first, baby."

She was bending over the table, picking up the rack off the balls, and I swear that she was teasing me. She knew what she was doing, and as soon as we're done here, I was going to break her thick ass in.

"Stop shaking that ass, P. There's nothing good that's going to come out of this."

"What are you tryna do to me?" she whispered in my ear while lickin' on my earlobe. "You think we can have the place to ourselves? I know your big money in these streets and money makes anything happen, right?"

"Aye Mickie, clear this bitch out. I need some private time." She laid her head on my shoulder while Mickie got everyone out.

"You good to go, boss!" he called out while he went to the back of the house.

I turned towards P to see just how ready she was. Lust filled her eyes as she eyed me down and licked her lips. Fuck it. I couldn't wait anymore. I needed to have her. That peanut butter colored skin, slim waist, and plump ass of hers get me every time.

"Come here," I urged while picking her up and placing her on the table. I placed a sloppy kiss on her lips while her hands traveled up and down my back. I tried to slip my hands under her shirt, but she stopped me. I didn't pay any attention to it as I tried again.

"Slow down. You're killing the foreplay. Just kiss me for a second." She started kissing me again, and I couldn't resist at this point. I grabbed a handful of her ass and tongued her down.

"Kindred always said that pretty bitches were your weakness." I turned around to see who it was and when I did, I was met with a blow to the head by the butt of a gun.

❦

WHEN I OPENED MY EYES, I TRIED TO REMEMBER WHAT HAPPENED. My head was banging while blood dripped down my face. As I reached to touch my head, I soon realized that my hands were tied behind my back. I had been caught slacking.

"Paisley? Baby, are you here? Are you hurt?" My heart sunk at the very thought of something happening to her.

"You might want to catch the company you keep," a voice called out from the distance. Then the sound of boots hitting the concrete floors caught my attention.

"Who the fuck are you?"

I needed my vision to come into play quickly. I needed to know who in their right fuckin' mind would do some shit like this. Damn near everyone knew who I was and wouldn't dare cross me.

"I heard you've been looking for me. Well, here I am." Low and behold, Ani stood in front of me looking just like Kindred. Her eyes held fire in them, and her body language exuded that of a killer.

"Yeah, glad you could make it niece. Why don't you go ahead and untie me so that we can settle this evenly?"

"Even before death, you speak with a foul tongue."

She stood before me with her arms crossed over her chest and a mean mug to match how she truly felt. I knew that if I didn't get to her, then she would get to me. Messing around with Paisley had me off my game.

"Before you take me out, I just need to know if Paisley is okay. She's all I care about. Don't hurt her on my account. I'll deal with my punishment on my own."

"Paisley!" Ani called out. A sigh of relief came out when I saw Paisley walk next to Ani unharmed. "Thank you for all of your help, sweetie. We couldn't have done this without you."

"Girl, it wasn't a problem at all, but I'm gonna need an extra bag since the old man decided to feel me up." She rolled her eyes while Ani laughed.

"I got you, ma. Mickie showed me the surveillance. I'm so sorry that you had to endure that, but you my bitch for real." They hugged it out, and Paisley blew a kiss my way and winked.

"Fuck you, bitch! Fuck you!" Damn, how the fuck did I let my guard down like this? I'm usually on top of shit like this, but I'm a sucker for a fat ass and a pretty smile. If I make it out of here, I seriously need to reevaluate my choices.

"You ain't gettin' outta here so you can shake that thought. You've tried to kill me on more than one occasion. After today, there won't be a nigga walkin' this earth that'll be able to say that. When I'm done fuckin' with you, you're going to be begging me to kill you. Let's get started."

"I should have killed you when I had the chance," I spoke through gritted teeth. If I were going to go out, then I would go out the way I saw fit. I wasn't going to go out like no bitch.

"You truly don't know when to shut the fuck up. I've grown quite tired of you Nolton, and I have no desire to prolong this situation. I was going to draw this shit out but I'm hungry, and I'm tired. Plus, I have bigger shit to deal with. Enjoy hell."

She drew her gun from behind her back and sent three slugs into my body. My body flew back and slammed against the concrete. Blood poured from the sides of my mouth as I searched for an ounce of breath. The walls were closing in on me, and all I could do at this point was ask the Lord to forgive me of my sins.

❧ 33 ❧

CAMILLE DE LINA

Owen thought that he could continue to disrespect me and nothing would happen. That was far from the truth. I've always had my suspicions about there being another woman. I just never had any proof. Seeing the way that Owen looked at Ani when she walked in his hospital room gave me all the confirmation that I needed.

He thought that our trip to LA was for us to relax and rekindle our relationship. That was far from the truth. I needed help resolving this situation, and the only person that could help was my father.

"Daddy!!!" I yelled through the house.

I wouldn't call myself a spoiled brat, but I got mainly everything I wanted and more from my father. When I called, he came running. It's been that way since I was a little kid and it wasn't going to stop.

"Cami, why are you yelling like you've lost your mind?" He came down the stairs not looking a day over thirty-five. Nikolas De Lina was every woman's dream— handsome and wealthy.

"I need your help with something."

"Is that the only time you come to visit me, Cami? You only come down here when you've gotten yourself into some trouble, or you want me to help you figure something out. You never come to spend time with your old man. What's up with that?" His face showed genuine signs of disappointment.

I never wanted to disappoint my father. It's just that I couldn't handle being around him for more than a few days. Whenever I was around him, he would try to set me up with one of his partners' sons because it would be good for the business. I never understood why I had to do this for the business. We were in a good position money wise and didn't need a damn thing from anyone.

"You know why I haven't been here, daddy. I've just been keeping a low profile and enjoying life in Chicago."

"No, you've been avoiding me because you think that I'm trying to arrange a marriage for you. That's far from the truth, Cami. I'm just trying to make sure that you are set for life. I'm not always going to be here to make sure that you're good."

"Dad, stop. I'm going to be okay. I promise. No, Owen doesn't make tons of money, but he started a new job, and he's doing well for himself. Actually, that's why I'm here. Owen—"

My father took a deep frustrated breath.

"Anyways, I need your help finding some information on a woman by the name of Ani Mack. Can you help me with that?"

At first, he hesitated, but then he gave in and called up one of his guys. A few minutes later, he came into the living room and took a seat on the couch next to me.

"Cami, you need to leave that woman alone! Don't go near her. Do you understand me? I also feel that it's best for you to leave Owen as well." My father seemed visibly shook, and for the life of me, I couldn't understand why.

"But why? Who is she and why has she ruined my life!"

"Baby girl, she's the daughter of Kindred Edwards. That should be more than enough to leave that woman be."

Never in my life had my heard my father speak to me like this about someone. Time and time again, he said that the only person that he feared was God. Right now, that doesn't seem to be the case.

"Since when does anyone in this family fear someone other than God. I know Nikolas De Lina's is not afraid of a little girl!"

"Camille, you have no idea what you're up against. Leave her alone. That is an order."

I grabbed my purse and walked out of the door. I don't know what the fuck my father thinks this is, but I am no longer a little girl. He will not order me around. I stomped out of the door and ran into Esteban.

"Woah, slow down baby. I know you've been anxious to see me." Esteban was one of the men my father tried to pair me up with. Apparently, he worked under my father and was doing good for himself. In all honesty, I wanted nothing to do with him, but as he stared me in my face, I was rethinking his value in my life.

"I'm sorry, Esteban. I would have dressed up if I had known you were here."

Just because daddy wasn't going to help me, didn't mean that I wouldn't be able to find someone else to do it. Esteban was the perfect person. He's wanted me since before I started my relationship with Owen. It was going to be a breeze to get him on my team.

"Oh baby, you look perfectly fine." He licked his lips seductively. "When you gonna let me take you out, Cami?"

"Hmm, how does tomorrow night sound? Pick me up from here at nine?" With my finger, I traced along his jawline, and it flexed. He was right where I needed him to be.

"T-tomorrow night s-sounds good." His stuttering was a clear indication that I will have him eating out the palm of my hand tomorrow night. "Dress to impress, baby. I'm going to give you a night you'll never forget." I kissed his cheek and continued out the door.

I had to figure out what excuse I was going to use to get out of the house tonight. Honestly, I'm not even sure I would need an excuse. Owen wasn't paying any attention to me anyway. It's okay because as soon as I find out as much information about Ani, I was going to rid my relationship of that problem.

৩৫৩

JUST AS I EXPECTED, OWEN SHOWED NO INTEREST IN MY EXCUSE TO get out of the house tonight. He claimed that he wasn't feeling well when I asked him to join me. I prayed that he hasn't switched up and decided at the last minute to go with me. As soon as the words left his mouth, I bolted out of the door.

The drive to my father's beach house was only fifteen minutes from the house where Owen and I were staying. When I pulled into the gates, Esteban was already there. He and my father were standing on the front stairs having some sort of discussion. From the looks of it, my father was not interested in whatever he had to say. I parked the car, check my lip gloss out in the mirror, and then stepped out. He said dress to impress and that's exactly what I did.

I stepped out of the car wearing a blush, off the shoulder Heath Ledger dress that hugged every inch of my perfectly sculpted body. Esteban's mouth fell open when he saw me. My father had yet to look my way, but that all changed when he realized that he was talking to a brick wall.

"Hey Nik, my date's here. I gotta get going. I'll hit you up when it's time to re-up." Esteban tried to shake my father's hand, but that didn't go as planned. He shook it off and came down the steps to greet me. He kissed my cheek and continued to gawk over me.

"Have a good night, daddy," I said while winking at him and getting in the car.

What my father fails to realize is that I get everything that I want. And right now, all I want is for Ani Mack to leave Owen and I alone... by any means necessary.

༺ 34 ༻

MARIYAH MACK

"You know Ani's is going to start asking questions if we don't tell her what's going on. She sees the black car pull into the gate every time you pick me up. She's already suspicious, and sooner rather than later, she is gonna bust us."

For the past few days, I've been sneaking out of the house to meet up with an old friend. I never thought that I'd be sneaking around like I wasn't the mother in this situation.

"Ha, Ani's a piece of work. She'll be okay with not knowing who I am for a little while longer. How have you been though?"

Just hearing his smooth baritone voice caused a smile to form on my face. He reached across the table and caressed my hand with his thumb. I politely removed my hand from his grasp and grabbed hold of my wine. The glass touched my lips, and I took in a small amount. In reality, I was trying to hide the subtle smile forming on my lips. It's been a long time since a man had me feeling this way.

"You ask me this every time you see me. I'm doing fine. Not much has changed since our date last night."

"Aye, I'm just tryna make sure you're good."

Silence filled the air around us as we searched each other's eyes. What was I doing? Was this really a road that I wanted to go down? I danced back and forth between these questions, but deep down, I knew that this was where I needed to be.

"How did you get out?"

"I have my ways." He flashed that smile at me, and I damn near melted in the seat.

If Ani knew that I was sneaking around having dinner dates with none other than Kindred Edwards, she would flip her lid. She was definitely going to lose it all when she found out that he was out for good. I've been begging him to tell me how he got out, but he was not budging. Apparently, the less I knew, the better off I was.

"When are we going to tell her?"

"When the time is right, Riyah. For now, I want her to continue doing things her way. I don't want to step back onto the scene and then her lieus not respect her anymore. I heard she had a problem with one of them already. How's Manny livin' these days?"

It was now his turn to place the glass full of scotch to his lips, while I was stuck here speechless. Only a select few people knew what happened to Manny. Questions were raised throughout the streets, but from what we've placed out there, he fucked over the wrong woman. No one knew of him and Ani's relationship, and we intend to keep it that way.

"How do you know everything?"

"Like I said I have my ways. I still run these streets, Mariyah. Remember that."

"Okay Mr. Edwards, since you still run these streets, what can you tell me about Nikolas' little girl? Is she something that we have to worry about, or is she harmless?" Ever since that night at the hospital, I've been trying to find out as much information about Owen's girlfriend as I could. Since I've been out of the game for so long, it's been hard for me to be discreet and get information. I could have asked the people on Ani's team, but they would have reported to her with my findings. My next step was to go to Kindred to get the information. However, when I called the jail, I found out that he had been released.

"Shit, I don't know about her. Nik and I have had the treaty in place for a few years, so I don't know much about her. I can dig around and see what I can find. Why are you lookin' for that information?"

I hadn't told him about Ani and Owen, nor do I plan on doing so any time soon. That was not my story to tell whatsoever. Kindred missed out on twenty-two years of her life. Now that he's out, he's going to do everything in his power to try to take care of her. That means going as far as checking up on her boyfriends. I knew about Owen's past from Tony, and all in all, I feel that he's a good guy. I just wasn't ready to throw him to a wolf like Kindred.

"No reason in particular," I mumbled. At first, I thought he bought it, but then when he pulled out his phone, I knew right then and there I had fucked up.

"Aye Tone, you would tell me if Ani was messin' with a nigga, right?" He placed the phone on speaker, and I prayed to God Tony didn't sell her out.

"Why? You tryna figure out who's got my niece's head gone?"

"I'll catch up with you later, Tone. We'll discuss it when I'm not around company."

"Ooooh hey, Riyah!" he yelled out while laughing.

Instead of responding, I rolled my eyes and continued to sip from my glass of wine. Kindred took the phone off speaker and continued small talk with Tony. During that time, the server had placed our food on the table, and soon after, I was digging into it.

"You're really not going to tell me why you need this info on Niko-las?" It was now my turn to sit in silence. "Wow, okay. It must be seri-ous. I'll see if I can hit up some of my old connects to see if they can find out her danger level. Is there anything else that I can do for you, Ms. Mack?" He reached over the table and caressed my jawline with his thumb. A chill shot through my body as I closed my eyes and bit my bottom lip.

"You have a lot of lost time that you need to make up." He gave a slight smirk and signaled for the server to bring the check.

"Anything to make you happy Riyah," his professed while placing soft kisses on my hand.

This was the man that I fell in love with. He was smooth, charm-ing, and put my needs before anything else. Kindred was my soulmate no matter how we tried to flip the deck. Even after all this time, I knew that there was no place else that I'd rather be.

35

BRITTON MATTHEWS

"D J stop, we can't do that right here!" I tried to wiggle out of his grasp. However, my strength was no match for his. He continued to hold onto me tight while biting and nibbling on the back of my neck. "Babe, we're in public. Stop someone's going to see us."

"I don't give a fuck. I'll pay to have this place shut the fuck down if that means I get to touch and kiss on this good shit right here," he whispered forcefully in my ear. We were currently in an arcade, and I was trying to win at skee ball. However, he had other plans.

Ever since he came to my rescue after the incident with Nolton, I'd been giving him a little bit of my time. The only thing that I hadn't given him was *this good shit right here*. Baby boy was going to have to earn that, and taking me out on a few dates here and there wasn't going to cut it. I needed to see that he was willing to step back a little from the game in order to protect us and our future.

"Brit, I'm gonna have blue balls fuckin' with you. Just let a nigga put the head in."

"Boy, if you don't—" I fell out laughing at his antics. He was acting as if I had the map to El Dorado between my legs. "Sittin' here acting like a horny teenager. Get your shit in order."

His idea of getting his shit in order was attacking me with kisses and trapping me in a bear hug. These little gestures were helping me realize more and more why I had originally fallen in love with him. He is handsome, intelligent, charming, and most definitely makes me laugh. If I asked God right now to send me the perfect man, he would send me DJ.

"I guess this is why you turn down my advances," a voice from behind us called out. The voice was way too familiar for my liking.

When I turned around my suspicions were confirmed. Standing directly behind us, holding the hand of a toddler, was none other than Range. DJ still had me in a bear hug, and I could feel the tension in his muscles. If Range knew what was best for him, he would walk away and pretend like he doesn't know me. Shit, if he wasn't then I was.

"I'm sorry. Do I know you?" I questioned while trying to walk away. I don't know who I was trying to fool because DJ didn't buy into my act.

"The lady asked a question. Does she know you?" This shit was going to go downhill. If I didn't divert this situation, it was bound to get ugly. DJ's temper wasn't something that I wanted to be displayed in public.

"Yeah, she knows me. I'm one of her highest paying clients, and I must say that it's absolutely worth it since I get to see that ass in spandex and sports bras for sixteen whole sessions."

If I could disappear, I would have. Range was tap dancing on DJ's sanity, and it was going to be blood shed if I didn't defuse the situation.

"Ha, ha, jokes over. Thanks for saying hi Range, but I think it's best that you go." The little boy attached to his arm agreed with me. "It looks like your son is itching to enjoy the rest of his day. Focus on that."

"He's not my son, Britton. He's my nephew. The only child I'm trying to have is with you. That is whenever you decide to let me explore the gold mine that is in between—"

"If you finish that sentence...I promise they're gonna be wipin' ya brains off of the air hockey table." DJ's hand reached for his waist, and I had to stop him. Range is a high-profile lawyer, and the last thing we needed was him digging into DJ's background. "I suggest you take the lil homie to eat some pizza and play some games before you find your-self in some shit that you can't escape, playboy."

When DJ threatened Range with death, the look on his face was priceless. He didn't know what he had gotten himself into. Using his better judgment, he turned himself around and walked away from us.

Even though I paid no attention to Range's advances, DJ was still pissed. He released me from his hold and walked out of the arcade. I found a little girl and passed her the rest of our tokens and tickets. Her mother thanked me for my generosity, and when we were done, I went to search for DJ. When I got outside, I searched the parking lot three times for his car. To my surprise, it was nowhere to be found. I didn't even do anything, and I was being punished. If Range were anywhere near me right now, I'd strangle him. One thing I wasn't going to do was play games and waste my time. If DJ wanted to have an attitude, then he was going to have one all by himself.

"Hey boo, whatcha doing?" I cooed into the phone.

"What you need?" she said groggily into the phone.

"I need a huge favor. Wanna come pick me up? I'm kinda stuck at the moment."

"Send the location." She quickly hung up the phone, and I did exactly as I was told.

Fifteen minutes later, Ani came speeding into the parking lot. Yeah, I could have called an Uber, but I wouldn't have been able to gossip with the driver. Plus, I knew she would want to hear all of this in person. I slid in the car and waited for her to pull off. When she didn't, I looked at her sideways.

"What are we waiting for?"

"I'm waiting on you to tell me why you woke me up out of my good sleep. And why the hell are you at an arcade?"

"It's a long story, and I don't want to talk about it." I curled up in a ball in the passenger seat and closed my eyes. I wanted to see how far I could push her buttons before she got upset.

A few minutes passed before she slapped my thigh with her tiny hands. "Aye, what was that for?" I jumped up out of the seat like I was shocked.

"Brit, you better tell me what the hell is going on before I catch a whole attitude." I sat up in the seat and decided to finally tell her everything that happened. When I finished, she continued to look straight ahead as if she was processing everything.

"I see Range has a death wish. There are a few reasons as to why DJ left your ass there. The first reason being, you didn't tell him in advance that you had a male client on your tail. That makes him feel as if you're trying to hide shit from him. The second reason would be because you didn't introduce him as your man. You didn't set Range completely straight, and that's why he's feeling some kind of way. Ya fucked up, mama. Now, it's up to you to figure out if you want to fix it. You love that man, and for the sake of everyone's sanity, I need you and him to get back right."

I hated that she was right. No matter how I hard I tried to fight it, I was still in love with him. Someway, somehow, I need to make things right with him.

"What do you suggest I do?"

"Do you think you'll be able to get into his apartment?" That's when I remembered that his sister handed me her business card. I wonder if she'd be willing to help. She told me to make it right with him, and that's exactly what I plan on doing.

"Hey Skylar, it's Britton. Do you have a minute?" My stomach turned into knots as I waited for her response. She's not my biggest fan at the moment, so I didn't know how this was going to play out.

"Britton, I'm surprised to receive a call from you. What can I help you with?"

"Before I tell you what happened, I just want to say that I appreciate you taking my call. I know that I'm not your favorite person. However, I messed up, and I need your help."

"I'm willing to help, but I need to know all of the details. Are you able to meet up for drinks? I'm free now." The fact that she was willing to help put me in a much better mood.

"Yeah, I'm free now. Just tell me the place. Also, I'm bringing a friend." She said it was perfectly fine and sent me the location of the bar. Ani was down to help me fix everything, and that's why I appreciated her.

We arrived at the location within thirty minutes. Sitting in the corner as promised was Skylar. Even though it was dark inside the bar, you could tell that she was a beautiful woman. She was older, maybe in her mid to late thirties. She and DJ were polar opposites in the looks department. DJ skin was smooth and dark like the night, and her skin was golden and glowing like the morning sun. She must have felt me staring at her. Her head popped up, and she waved us down.

As we made our way across the bar, a funny feeling rumbled in my stomach. I'm not much into listening to my gut, but this was a feeling that I couldn't shake. I wrapped my arm in Ani's and held on to her as we made our way back.

"Hey ladies, glad you could make it." Skylar stood up from the seat and opened her arms for hugs. "Come on. I'm a hugger. Plus, we had a rough start. I want to make sure that we're good."

"It's all good. I just want to thank you for taking the time out to meet with me. And you're right...we had a rough start, and I'm sorry for that. Your brother means so much to me that it hurts sometimes."

"Trust and believe me. I know exactly what you mean. However, I haven't had a man in a while. Work keeps me busy. I'm sorry. I'm rambling. And who is this gorgeous chocolate cutie?" she questioned while taking in Ani and her features.

"My bad, this is my best friend, Ani. Ani this is Skylar, DJ's sister." They said their pleasantries, and then we sat down. The server came over, took our drinks, and returned with them shortly.

We started to talk about different ways that I could fix the relationship that hasn't even started. Things were going well, but I couldn't ignore that feeling in my gut any longer.

"You ever get that feeling like someone is watching—"

I wasn't able to finish my sentence before a man approached the table. We all stopped talking and took in his appearance. He was a Hispanic male, standing at about six foot five, with a typical pretty boy face.

"E-excuse me, I-I'm sorry to bother you ladies, but I wanted to know if I could buy you a drink."

"No thank you, I'm still working on this one," I spoke up and turned my attention back to Ani and Skylar.

"Forgive me. I wasn't speaking to you. I was actually speaking to the Nubian goddess." He winked at Ani and then smiled. Shit, he didn't have to tell me twice. I took a sip from my drink and looked at Ani's face.

"I'm sorry. Do I know you?"

"No, you don't, but if you give me a chance, we can fix that."

"Damn, you're bold. You're really going to spit game in front of us?" Skylar sipped from her glass of wine and sized him up.

"Nah, I'm good. Thanks for showing interest though."

"Damn, a nigga can't get no play in these Chicago streets," he mumbled while walking away. "Let me take my ass back to California where the bitches have more respect for a fly ass nigga like myself."

"Aht, aht. Simmer down, lil daddy. Take your "L" and keep it pushin'. There's no need to get disrespectful." Ani's grip tightened around her glass as she stared him down. He ended up flipping her off and walking out the door of the bar.

"Damn Ani. You make friends wherever you go." It was now her turn to flip the bird at me.

The rest of our time there went well. Sky immediately clicked with us, and it was nice hearing someone a little older than us give us some good advice. She really helped me figure out just how I was going to get back on track with DJ. I just gotta wait for my package to arrive from Amazon.

"It was so nice chilling with you ladies." Sky gleamed while we stood on the sidewalk outside of the bar. "We have to do this more often. I don't have many girlfriends out here in Chicago."

"Is this move permanent for you?" Ani asked the question that I had been dying to ask. I needed to know what she and DJ were going to do. If he was willing to stay here, then that was going to make things that much sweeter.

"Well, it seems like my little brother has a good reason to stay here. I shouldn't be telling you this, but he's been looking at properties here."

Before I was able to show an ounce of excitement, a van pulled up quickly at the end of the block. Sky and Ani's backs were to them, so they weren't able to see what I was seeing. The door flew open, and three men holding semi-automatics jumped out and started spraying the street. The three of us ducked behind the few parked cars lined against the street and pulled guns from our purses. It amazed me how all three of us were strapped. Skylar was the one that shocked me the most.

"Move, let's see if we can make it back to the bar!" Ani yelled while letting off a few shots. Glass was shattering everywhere around us. The longer we waited, the quicker we were going to meet death. "Duck and cover each other."

We all took deep breaths and then the shooting stopped. They were reloading. "Let's go."

The three of us popped up and started making our way back to the bar. Ani got the man closes to us, and Sky got the guy next to him since he was caught off guard by his friend going down. The last shooter was now reloaded and staring us in our face.

"Fuck! I'm out of bullets!" Sky yelled.

A smile reached the shooter's eyes as he fired off a shot towards her. Everything around me was moving in slow motion. I swear I hope that DJ knows just how much I love him... I pushed Sky to the ground and felt the bullet rip through my shoulder and arm. Thankfully, I was able to fire off a shot, and it hit him dead in his head. We fell to the ground at the same time.

36

ANI MACK

I need someone to tell me something right now. I'm sitting in this emergency room a nervous wreck. The doctors weren't telling me anything, and if they kept this up, then I was liable to nut the fuck up. Britton and I had only known each other for a few years, and I'd grown to love her like she was my sister. We were different from one another, but still similar in other ways. If she didn't pull through, then I didn't know how I was going to survive.

My phone rang, and I wanted to throw it across the room. Word of tonight's incident spread quickly through the street, and everyone wanted to know what the hell happened. I could give two fucks about who did it and why it happened right now. My sole focus was figuring out if Brit was going to make it. I'll deal with the people responsible once I heard from the doctor.

Skylar's soft whimpers in the corner softened me a little bit. She froze in front of the shooter, and I know she feels responsible for Brit taking a bullet for her. Fuck, I forgot to call DJ and let him know what happened. Here I am sitting here worrying about *me* when he had the right to know about her condition. He could be mad at her all he wants, but right now, he was going to have to put that aside and come see her before it was too late.

I went to dial his number, and before I could press send, the emergency room doors flew open, and he came running in, followed by Owen, my mom, and Tony. *Damn, word really does travel through these streets quickly.* We had only been at the hospital for about fifteen to twenty minutes. How the hell did all of them arrive at the same time?

My mother scanned the emergency room, and her eyes met mine. She raced over to me with everyone on her tail. I just held my head back to keep the tears from falling. Times like these made me wish that I had never gone to the courthouse that day. Kindred would have never known about me, and I would be living my normal ass life at the library right now. That's exactly where I wanted to disappear to right now. The solace and comfort of the library was needed in order for me to regain some peace of mind.

"Ani, is something wrong with you? Can you hear me?" My mother had been yelling my name and shaking me for about twenty seconds. I had completely zoned out while thinking about escaping my current reality.

"Yeah ma, I can hear you, even though I'm not trying to right now." I tried mumbling the last part. She heard me, and that's when her hand connected to my shoulder. "Ah, what you hit me for?" I opened my eyes and sized her up.

"Don't get smart with me Ani'Yah! What the hell happened tonight? And who is this over here crying?" She fired off while pointing to Skylar.

"Sky? Why the fuck you here? You were involved with this?" Chatter erupted amongst everyone, and I wanted nothing more than all of them to shut the hell up.

"Aye, I'm gonna need everyone to sit down and shut the fuck up, sorry no disrespect, ma." She cocked her head to the side but remained silent. "Once everyone takes their seat, I'll be able to explain everything that went down."

Everyone sat down except for Owen, who I had completely forgotten was there. He remained standing and leaned against the wall with his arms folded. I tried to look away, but his mannerism and body language pulled me into his presence. There was that I wanted nothing more right now than to run in his arms and fall out crying.

"Today? You gonna tell us what happened, today?" DJ clapped his hands at me.

"Aye chill out D, we wouldn't be in this situation if you hadn't—" I took a deep breath. It wouldn't be right for me to place blame on anyone right now.

"Nah gone finish that statement, Ani. If I hadn't what?"

"Little brother, we wouldn't have been in this position if you hadn't let your attitude get the best of you at the arcade. You left her there, and then Ani came to pick her up! She was so distraught by you leaving that she was willing to do any and everything to make it up to you. That's when she called me asking for help on what to do to get back in your good graces. She took those bullets for me! I froze in front of the last shooter, and she pushed me out of the way. That should be me in there right now." Skylar ran off in tears as DJ sat there visibly upset. However, his eyes showed a bit of remorse.

"S-she was going to what?" His voice cracked.

"We only met up with Sky so that she could figure out how to make this up to you. The girl lying on that operating table loves you more than life itself, and she realized that a long time ago. She was willing to do whatever it took to get y'all back right. This shit hasn't been easy for her by far, and she just wanted to fix it. I'm not trying to blame you by far DJ, but I need you to understand why we were all out in the first place."

He sat back in his chair and rested his head against the wall. Tears slid down his face, and Skylar walked back in the room, sat next to him, and gently wiped them away. Emotions were running high on all ends. Anxiety ripped through me with every passing second. I needed to hear something soon. If I didn't, then was going to end up in the psych ward.

"Who the hell had a problem with the three of y'all?" Tony asked, breaking the silence. "Did anything out of the ordinary happen tonight?" I hadn't put much thought into who could be responsible for the incident. With Nolton being gone, I didn't know who could be responsible for this.

"No, it was a normal night. We were only there for about an hour or so. It was really a regular night. Guys hit on us and all." Fuck, how could I have missed that? The guy that hit on me was super mad that I didn't give him the time of day.

"There was this one gentleman that was rather upset that Ani didn't want anything to do with him," Skylar spoke up.

"Aye, what's his name?" Owen had now joined the conversation.

"Shit, we never got that far. He asked if he could buy a drink. I shot him down, and he said that he was gonna take his ass back to California." Owen's face scrunched up, and he pulled out his phone.

"Excuse me, I'm looking for the family of Britton Matthews," a short older black woman with silver hair called out.

"That'll be us." I pointed to everyone in the room.

"Hello, I'm Dr. Young." She paused and scanned the room. "Owen? Owen Pierce is that you?" Everyone turned their heads to Owen, and he gave her a simple head nod. "I-I'm sorry. Where was I... ah yes. Ms. Matthews. Two bullets penetrated her body. However, they were through and through. She's one of the lucky ones and will make a full recovery. She should be waking up shortly, and then we'll have the nurses escort you all back two at a time."

I thanked her for all of her help and took a seat while waiting for the nurse to come out.

"Excuse me, Owen. Can I speak to you for a moment?" Owen took a deep breath as he and the doctor stood off to the side.

My eyes never left them as I was dying to know what they had to talk about. Dr. Young placed her hand on his shoulder as his head fell and his chin touched his chest. A deep heavy sigh lifted his body up and then brought it back down. Whatever she revealed to him was obviously something that he wasn't prepared for. Before they separated, she wrapped him up in a motherly hug and patted his back. She left out of the emergency room, and Owen took a seat in a chair across the way.

It took everything in me to not jump out of my seat, wrap my arms around him, and let him know that it was going to all be okay. I wanted to let him know that no matter happens, I'll always be there for him. Just as I was about to get up and walk over to him, my mother sat next to me and placed her hand on my knee.

"Sweetie, give him some time."

"W-what do you mean, mommy?"

I knew exactly what she meant. She was stopping me from making a fool of myself in this hospital. At the end of the day, the fact still remained, Owen was a man that was off limits to me. From what I've heard, he's still very much in a relationship with *her*.

"You know exactly what I'm talking about, Ani. Your love for him may be there, but it's probably not the right time. Be there to support him, but that's it, no more. When it's time for y'all to be together, then you'll know."

I wanted to fight her and everything she was saying. However, there was no use. She was one hundred percent right about it all. Maybe it's best for me to get over Owen and the one night we shared.

"I know it's hard, baby. Just think of it like this, who's to say that you guys won't find your way back to each other?" She winked at me and patted my leg before walking away.

"Family of Britton Matthews. We're going to start taking two at a time. Who would like to go first?" DJ's head popped up at the sound of her name. Tears welled in the bottom of his eyes and caused my heart to ache for him. Part of me believed that all of this could have been avoided. However, I'm not entirely sure. I needed to figure out who was ordered the hit.

"DJ, you and Sky can go ahead. I'm gonna go get some air, and I'll be back in a little while. Let my girl know that I love her, and I'll be back soon." He nodded, and Sky kissed my cheek.

"See ya soon, chica," she said before they walked past the double doors.

When I turned around, I noticed my mother and Tony were in the corner of the emergency room having a heated discussion. From her body language, she was going off on him about something. If I had to guess, it would have been about my security. I had told Reggie to fall back when I left to get Brit. He didn't need to follow me around the city when it was for something as simple as that. I'm sure my mother felt a different way about that now. I walked towards them to defend Reggie, but I was met with words that I'd never thought that I'd hear.

"Ani, how much of that did you hear?" my mother quizzed. Her eyes feverously searched mine for an answer.

"I heard enough to hear that Kindred is out and it seems to me like he's been out for some time. Shit, it wasn't gonna hurt me for you to tell me."

Both my mother and Tony stood before me with dumbfounded looks on their faces. It seems as though I wasn't supposed to find out about this.

"Ani," my mother opened her mouth. However, I held up my hand in protest. They had their reasons for not telling me, and deep down, I wasn't even upset. I had too many things on my plate to worry about. Kindred being out of those prison walls wasn't going to change a thing.

"It's all good. I'm not even mad, mom. You guys did what you thought was best, and I appreciate that. If you'll excuse me, I'm gonna set outside for a minute."

Before they could stop me, I exited the emergency room doors. Rain fell from the sky above and pounded down on my body. I turned my head up towards the sky and let the tears that I had been holding in fall. I thought that I would be able to contain them and only allow two or three to fall. However, I was wrong. Tears fell out of my eyes by the boatload, and there was nothing that I could do to stop it. I was crying so hard, that I began to hyperventilate. If I didn't regain control over my breathing, I was going to be in a world of trouble.

I kneeled down towards the ground and grabbed hold of my chest. The harder I tried to labor my breathing the more I panicked. My mind and body were not on the same page, and I was bound to pass out if I kept this up. Just as a full-blown panic attack crept up on me, a pair of arms wrapped around me and helped me to my feet causing my body to fall at ease.

Two fingers swiped my face wiping away the tears that were now mixed with rain. I didn't have to look up and open my eyes to know who was holding me. Our souls had been tied to each other since the first night they met, and I knew that it was *him*. The same *him* that I had been secretly craving for and damn near losing my mind without. The fact that he was standing out here with me in the rain, soaking wet was enough for my heart to swell even more.

"You don't have to be out here. I'm fine," I lied. I wasn't fine by far.

However, I didn't want anyone worrying about me any more than they already were.

"I know I don't *have* to be out here Ani. I *want* to be." He tilted my head up towards him, but I kept my eyes tightly shut. "Why won't you look at me?"

"I-I just can't," I stumbled to get the words out of my mouth.

"What do you mean you can't?" He wasn't trying to hear the words out of my mouth. I was trying to save him from what would happen if I opened my eyes. If he knew what was good for him, he would leave me be. "Ani, open your damn eyes right now," he demanded.

Against my better judgment, I opened my eyes, allowing him to see me, yet again, in a vulnerable state. Owen has seen the softer more gentle side of me, far too many times for my liking. I didn't want him to think that I was a girl trapped in a woman's body because I couldn't handle the stresses of life. For a minute, we just stared into each other's eyes. No words were said, and not a judgement was made. The rain continued to beat down on us until he finally broke the silence.

"I miss—"

"Don't you dare. Don't you dare let those words come out of your mouth. Owen, we can't keep doing this to each other. The stolen glances suffice for the moment, but what happens when we start to want more? We've already done things that we shouldn't have."

"You didn't want that?" he said while stroking my chin. I couldn't fall deeper into his gaze. I really needed to put some distance in between us.

"Of course, I wanted it, but that doesn't excuse the fact that you're spoken for. And as long as you are, there can be no us." I pushed his hands from off of me and began walking back into the emergency room. DJ and Skylar should be done with their visit soon, and I'd be able to check on my girl.

"I found out how my father died," he called out behind me, causing me to stop dead in my tracks. The night that his father passed, he rushed out of the hospital without finding out the cause of death or even grieving properly.

"W-what," I managed to muster out even with a lump occupying my throat. To this day, I hated that Owen left his father to come save me. It's something that I'll regret until the day that I die. "How?"

"Sadly, lung cancer." He started walking away from me, and I needed to stop him.

"Come see me tonight?" I blurted out. He stopped walking and turned to face me. In the blink of an eye, he ran up to me and planted a passionate kiss on my lips. The kiss was so intense that it took my breath away.

"Go check on your girl. I'll see you later," he said as he released my face from his hold.

I stood in complete shock as he walked away into the darkness of the night. The further he was from me, the less and less I was able to breathe. From one simple night, Owen Pierce had my heart, my soul, and my breath in his hands. Was this what love felt like for everyone?

When I walked into the emergency room, all eyes were on me. My clothes and hair were soaking wet. I was out here resembling a lost child. My mother and Tony had dumbfounded looks on their face. I held up my hand to stop them from opening their mouths. There wasn't anything that anyone could say to me right now.

37

ANI MACK

When I arrived back to the estate, I noticed that the light to my room was on. The only person that could have been here right now was Owen. My mom and Tony had left the hospital before I came out of Britton's room. I'm almost sure they went to tell Kindred that I had learned of his return. My brain had so much going through it that I couldn't even process him being out. I'd deal with that at a much later date.

Arriving at my bedroom, I hesitated before opening the door. He was here to talk to me about his father— nothing more, nothing less. If things started heading *south,* then I was going to have to stay strong and get us back on track. At the end of the day, Owen was a man in a relationship, and we couldn't allow things to go any further.

Opening the door, I noticed that he was sitting on the couch with his head resting against the wall. His eyes were closed, and a light snore escaped his lips every few seconds. I didn't know whether to wake him up or leave him be. I needed to get out of these wet clothes, so I decided to leave him be and take a quick shower.

I tiptoed to the bathroom as quietly as I could so that I didn't disturb him. During his time as my bodyguard, I've never seen him sleep. No matter what time of the day I moved, he was up and moving right behind me.

"You gonna walk past a nigga like I can't hear your heartbeat, Ani?" The sound of his voice scared the shit out of me, and I ran into the wall.

"Fuck!" I screamed out while rubbing my sore forehead.

"That's what you get for tryna sneak past me."

"I wasn't trying to sneak past you," I sassed. "I've never seen you sleep before, so I decided to leave you be while I get out of these clothes."

He rubbed his chin and nodded his head. "Gone head and take a shower. I'll be here when you're done."

I probably took the quickest shower known to man. I literally hopped in, washed the necessary parts, and hopped the fuck out. When I walked back into the room, Owen chuckled.

"Ain't shit funny." I found myself laughing with him. What's done is done, I'm clean, and that's all that mattered. "You gonna tell me what's going on, or are you going to sit there and stare at me while I get dressed?"

"Real talk, I just wanna chill with you for a second. Come over here." His eyes were low and red. He was either really tired or really high.

"Okay, just let me lotion up and throw on some clothes."

"Ma, throw on a robe or something. You ain't gonna keep it on for too long anyway." He let out a low chuckle, and my mouth dropped. Yeah, Owen had smoked some of Chicago's finest bud before he got here.

I ignored his words and threw on an oversized hoodie and a pair of leggings. Walking to the couch, I tucked my leg in and tried to sit next to him. He then grabbed hold of me and sat me down on his lap instead. His arms were wrapped around my waist, and he nestled his head in the crook of my neck. With my thumb, I caressed his wrist and waited for him to talk. If he wanted to stay like this all night, then I was going to let him. For the next few minutes, we sat in complete silence until I heard a deep sigh come from the depths of his soul.

"The doctor told me that my father had been battling lung cancer for a while and didn't want me to know about it."

"Owen, I'm so sorry." I turned to face him, but he tightened his grip around me, making me realize that this was his safe space.

"Ani, that's not what killed him." His breathing became labored, and his body started heating beneath me.

"Talk to me, what killed him?"

He started talking, and I held my breath. His body began to shake underneath me, and it was starting to scare me. I had never seen him like this before. "The doctor said that his toxicology report came back, and he had a high dose of fentanyl in his system." If I was hearing this correctly, Owen just told me that someone killed his father.

"W-what? Who would do this to you?"

"Someone that's threatened by everyone in my life."

With my hand, I placed it under his chin and brought his eyes to mine. Seeing his face helped me understand why he didn't want me to move. It was stained with tears. I'd never seen Owen cry, other than the night his father passed, and it brought on a pain that I had never experienced in my life. The man that I had grown to know and love was always strong and confident. There was never a moment where he exhibited a hint of weakness. Seeing him in such a vulnerable state made me fall deeper in love with him.

"Why would she do this to you?" Tears welled in the bottom of my eyes as I tried to think of a logical reason for her to do this to him.

"I don't know, but I plan on finding out as soon as I get a hold of her. I've been trying to reach her since I left the hospital."

"Don't worry. I'll see what I can do. I didn't know your father, and I'm heartbroken that I didn't get a chance to meet him. However, I love you, and I promise that I'm going to do everything I can."

"You love me?"

I didn't realize that the words had slipped out. I opened my mouth to respond, but a lump was caught in my throat. I had been holding onto that for far too long. I knew I loved him the day that he came to save me from Manny. The way that he held me was so gentle and soft.

Finally, I took a deep breath and tried it again. "Yes. Yes, I love you.

I've loved you ever since that..." The words stopped flowing as my mind drifted to that night.

"I love you too," he said while placing his hands on the sides of my face. He placed his forehead on mine and closed his eyes while taking in a deep sigh. "I'm not a man that typically believes in love at first sight, but damn...it's something about you."

Hearing him confess his love for me touched my mind body and soul. This was the man that I was going to marry. Owen has a hold on my heart, and I pray that he never lets it go.

38

CAMILLE DE LINA

Nothing pissed me off more than someone who couldn't finish a job and do it correctly. Esteban had one job and one job only, and it was to kill Ani Mack. Hearing that the attempt was unsuccessful had me fuming. No, I didn't heed my father's warning when it came to the Edwards Cartel, and I didn't feel any kind of way about it. I know what I want in life, and I'm not going to let anything stop me from getting that.

The night that Esteban and I went out, I laid the sex appeal on him thick. By the end of our date, I had him eating out the palm of my manicured hand. At first, he was completely against it. Apparently, the Edwards name held some kind of weight in the streets. However, I didn't give a damn about that. Once I put this pretty little mouth to work, he completely forgot why he was scared. Daddy had kept me away from the street side of the family business, but I held no fear in my heart for anyone. I'd rumble with the big dogs if I had to.

"Hello daddy, how are you on this lovely Sunday morning? How's the weather in California?" I cooed into the phone. Nikolas wouldn't have called on a Sunday morning unless he found out about my extracurricular activities. He was about to chastise me like I was a little girl again.

"What did you do?!" He yelled so loud in the phone that I had to move it away from my ear.

"Daddy, what are you talking about?" I tried to play dumb, but he wasn't falling for it.

"Camille, you don't know what you've done." For the first time in my life, I heard something in my father's voice— fear.

"What does he have on you, daddy? Why does this family have you so spooked? I know I don't have a bitch made nigga as a father. Not big bad Nik from the block."

"Cami, I've made mistakes in the past that have cost this family more than you could even fathom. You deliberately disobeyed my warnings, and I refuse to allow you to take this operation down with you. I've worked too hard to give you a comfortable life. It pains me to say this, but you are now on your own. You will have to face the consequences of the piss poor decisions on your own. Then you dragged Esteban into this as well. Shame on you, Cami. The De Lina family will not have any parts of this war. I wish you the best."

"Daddy, wait! What do you mean I'm in this by myself?" I waited for an answer, but it never came. He had hung up and left me out to dry.

After realizing that I was now by myself, I called Esteban's phone for some support. I needed to know the details of everything that happened last night. Since Ani is still alive and kicking, then I need to know if she would be able to link this back to me.

"Hello," Esteban answered the phone groggily.

"Esteban, what happened last night? How did Ani flee untouched?"

"Man, Cam, I lost two of my boys last night fuckin' with you and your stupid ass plan! Why you ain't tell me them pretty bitches were some sharpshooters? What the fuck have you gotten me into?" he yelled in the phone, and I had to move it from my ear.

"I'm going to need you to man up and calm down. Don't worry about what I've gotten you into. Just know that it'll be worth it when I convince my father to turn everything over to you when he retires. Now, back to Ani? How did she manage to get away untouched?"

"Man, the bitch got aim, Cami. Mami is nice, and she's about that gunplay. You may have bitten off more than you can chew with this one. She ain't ya average chica."

"Esteban, I don't give a fuck if she was a sharpshooter for the fuckin' marines. Ani Mack is going to pay for the havoc she's caused in my life. I hate her—" Before I could continue discussing my disdain for Ani, he cut me off.

"Hold up. Hold up. Bitch, did you just say Ani Mack? As in the Ani that took over for the Kindred "Big Kin" Edwards? Bitch is you crazy? Yup, you crazy."

"Excuse me? I'm not going to stay on this phone with you any longer if you're going to disrespect me."

"Mamacita, let me put you up on a little game since it seems as though all you did was spend daddy's money instead of figuring out how he made it. Kindred Edwards is the *only* reason Nikola has that little ass piece of the west coast. Word on the streets is Big Kin's older brother Kendrell was the biggest thing that the nation had seen since cocaine step on the streets in the '80s. Nik and Kendrell were the thickest of thieves growing up in Chicago. That is until Nik decided that he didn't want to be second best. Fast forward a few years...Nik ended up stealin' a couple of hundred bricks and fleeing to Cali."

I couldn't believe the story that Esteban was telling me. I never bothered to ask my father about his dealings with the family business. There were so many questions flying through my head as I continued to listen to him tell this story.

"You followin' me? Cool. Now, this is all just word from the streets, but I've heard this shit a few times, so I can only guess that it's real. Nik thought that shit was cool since Kendrell didn't come after him right away. He flipped those bricks and started up his little business or whatever. Kendrell knew all about Nik and his shit. Man, Kendrell was so fuckin' smooth with this next piece of info. Now, pay attention la princessa, this is where shit gets real. Kendrell agreed to let Nik keep his little business going on the west coast only if he sacrificed his greatest love." Silence fell over the phone as he took a long and dramatic pause.

"Esteban! Finish the story. What did he sacrifice?" My heart was in my throat as I waited for an answer. There were a plethora of things that my father could have sacrificed, and I need to know what kind of man he is.

"Mamacita, senora Gloriana was Nik's greatest love."

When he said that, the phone slipped out of my hand and came crashing to the floor. I hurriedly picked it up and hung up on him. That story couldn't have been true. It just couldn't have been. There was only one person that would be able to tell me the truth, and that was my father. I immediately called him back.

"Cami, there's nothing else that we need to discuss. I've made my—"

"Did you really kill my mother?" Tears streamed down my face as I yelled at him. I needed answers, and I needed them right now.

"As I said before, I've made mistakes that have caused this family a lot more than you'll ever know. Goodbye, Camille." He hung up the phone again, and all I could do was cry.

Ani will die. There's no other way for this to play out. Her family caused me to lose someone that I should have been able to call a best friend. However, I never got the chance. It was snatched from me, and I plan on snatching the very thing that is near and dear to the Edwards Cartel. However, I need to be smart about this. I've already marked myself as a target with Esteban's failed attempt, and from here on out, I have to move quickly and quietly.

39

MARIYAH MACK

"Kindred, I said I'm sorry. It was never either of our intentions for her to find out this way."

It's been a few days since the shooting, and it felt like the calm before the storm. In order for me to decompress, I came to have a little me time and get my hair done. Instead of relaxing, I was being berated like a teenage girl by her father. I understand Kindred's frustration about my little slip-up, but it wasn't the end of the fuckin' world. We had bigger fish to fry than that one.

"One thing I know for sure is that you better stop yelling at me. Ain't shit changed, Kin. I'm still the same Riyah that'll get down with the best of them."

"Aye, you sure talkin' tough shit like I won't pull up on you and get you right!" he yelled into the phone. One thing was for sure. Kindred had me messed up.

"Okay Kindred, if you say so. You don't even know where I am. You know what...I'm not about to argue with other people's children." I hung up the phone and continued to let my hairdresser do her thing.

While I was sitting under the dryer, the door to the salon swung open, and whispers began to surface. I heard everything from "damn" to "who is that" and "he's fine as hell." I continued to mind my business and check the emails on my phone. That is until someone stood in front of me with their arms crossed. The way the black t-shirt hugged onto his massive arms had my attention. The black jeans that hung slightly off his hips fit him too nicely. Kindred looked damn good, and every woman in this shop knew it.

"Damn, you look good today. Do you always wear six-inch red bottoms to get ya hair done?"

I used to be a gym shoe kind of girl, but as I got older, I hung those up and traded them in for any kind of heel that I could get my hands on. I didn't think I was doing too much today. I kept it as simple as possible. I wore a light-brown off the shoulder sweater, dark jeans, and black red bottoms.

"Mind your business, I'm a grown ass woman and will dress and act however I see fit." My eyes remained focused on my phone. Kindred didn't scare me.

"Riyah, why you like playing with me?" He squatted down in front of me and tried staring into the depths of my soul. This was a tactic that he used on me back in the day, but it would no longer work on me. At least that's what I thought.

"Kindred, you're making a scene. I'll be done in about an hour if you want to talk."

He swiped his hand down his face and licked his lips. A smirk crept up the left side of his face as he stood and lifted the hooded dryer off my hair. He leaned into the side of my face and whispered in my ear.

"I can make a scene, Mariyah. Is that what you want?"

His lips swiped against the side of my neck with every word. A chill traveled down my spine. A soft moan escaped my lips causing my face to flush bright red. He continued to place soft kisses on my neck, and I needed him to stop right now. I finally found my strength and pushed his face away from my neck.

"Yeah, I didn't think so," he confidentially stated as he stood up and straightened out his clothes. "Finish with this shit. I'll be outside in the car."

"W-wait, I drove my own car."

"I had it picked up!" he called out as he chucked the deuces and walked out the door. All I could do was sigh. Kindred was back on his regular bullshit. When the door closed, all eyes were on me.

"Chica, girl, can you finish me up before I catch a case in this bitch?" She quickly pulled me from under the dryer and finished my hair in record time. I thanked her and made sure to tip her a little extra.

When I walked outside, I saw the black Benz parked a few feet from the entrance. It was parked in front of a fire hydrant like he didn't give a damn that he could get ticketed or towed. I made my way over to the passenger side and started to open the door.

"Touch that door, and we're gonna have problems!" he yelled while stepping out of the car. I held my hands up in surrender and waited for him to walk over and open it. As I slid in, I made sure to face him while I rolled my eyes.

"Where is my car, Kindred?" I asked while folding my arms and throwing attitude his way. He ignored my question and continued to drive. "Where are we going, Kindred?"

"You're going with me. Just chill." I just shook my head, closed my eyes, and laid back in the seat. For the next ten minutes, we drove in complete silence.

"When do you think that she'll want to meet me up with me? Last time I saw her was while I was locked up. It's a different vibe when there's no glass." My eyes popped open, and I looked at the side of his face.

"Give her a chance to show you that she has love in her heart for you. Ani would have never come to the jail that morning if she didn't genuinely care about you and what you had to say. She's always been the type of person to figure out the answer to something. The fact that she came there for *your* help means that she's taking steps to work things out. You guys will be fine, Kindred." I leaned over the middle counsel and kissed his cheek.

"Thanks for giving me another chance." He grabbed my hand and placed soft kisses on the back of it.

"Who said anything about giving you another chance? Boy, you gotta work for this good shit." I snatched my hand out of his and fell out laughing.

"Aye Riyah, you gonna stop fuckin' playing with me." I was about to light his ass up until my phone started ringing. I held my finger up, signaling to give me one second.

"Hey Britton baby, how are you?"

"Ma, they took him away!" She sobbed into the phone.

"Brit slow down. Who did they take away? Where are you?"

"They took DJ! He was here at the hospital with me, and they swarmed in here on some hot shit. Threw him on the ground, roughed him up a bit, and hauled him away! I need you come get me. These dumb ass doctors won't let me sign myself. Mama Mack, I need you to come get me before I fu—"

"Slow down, Britton. I'm on my way. In the meantime, call the number I'm about to text to you. Tell her that I sent you and explain everything that just took place. I'm about twenty minutes away. Do I need to bring you some clothes?"

"No, ma'am. I'm good."

"Okay, calm down. I'll be there as soon as I can."

If it wasn't one thing, then it was another. We couldn't catch a break to save our lives. Kindred may have had plans for us, but unfortunately, those were going to have to wait. He immediately turned the car around and headed south to the hospital.

"Wait, where were you planning on taking me?"

"Don't worry about it." He had removed his hand from mine and was now using it to steer the car. His whole attitude had now shifted, and there wasn't anything that I could do about it.

Until he was able to articulate what was wrong with like a normal person, I was focused on helping Britton and DJ.

❧ 40 ❧

BRITTON MATTHEWS

"**O**ne thing for sure and two things for certain, you better believe that I'm leaving up out of this hospital ta-day! Do you understand me?"

Dr. Shabazz had me all the way fucked up. If they thought that I wasn't going to be in the first Uber smoking, then they had another thing coming.

Everything was going great today. DJ had been here at the hospital nonstop. Somehow, he managed to pay some people in order to let him stay. The only time he ever left this room was to grab some food or answer a call. Other than that, his tall ass was laying in this bed next to me.

"Britton, I heard you were in here acting a plum fool." My nurse stood at the door with her hands on her hips.

"Nah, I ain't acting a fool yet, but if they don't get me out of here, I promise to God that I'll nut the fuck up!" My voice elevated with every word. They were going to hear from me whether they liked it or not.

"Britton, acting a fool in here is going to get you a one-way ticket to the psych ward. Now explain to me what happened before I got here."

Nurse Rose began checking my vitals and redressing my wounds as I explained everything that happened. By the time I finished, all she could do was shake her head. If the police thought that they would get away with this, they were sadly mistaken. Their first mistake was not explaining to him his charges and not Mirandizing him before hauling his ass off.

Mama Mack gave me the number to a woman named Javi. I explained to her everything that happened, and she let me know that she would get right on it. Apparently, this was going to be open and shut, and the police department was going to wish they never fucked with us in the first place.

"Oh child, there's so much going on today. I don't know how y'all deal with all of this stress! I'm gonna pray for you and DJ because Lord knows y'all need it right now. I've grown quite fond of him during your time here."

I'd been stuck in this hospital for about a week, and if it weren't for Nurse Rose and DJ, I'd be sure to lose my damn mind. I thanked her for her prayers as she continued to check me out.

"You're all good sugar. I know that you probably have someone coming to bust you out of here, so I want you to take my number in case you need additional care. These wounds are still fresh and are going to take some time to heal. Be gentle with them, Britton. I don't want to see you back here with busted stitches." She wrapped her arms around me and hugged me.

"I packed some supplies for you in a bag and stuffed it with the rest of your belongings. You take care of yourself, do you understand me?" I nodded in acknowledgment before she walked out the door.

The loud buzzing of my cell phone caused me to jump up in fear. I was praying that it was Mama Mack calling to tell me that she was here. Looking at the caller ID, I noticed that it was from a private number. I rarely answered those on a normal day. However, this could have been DJ calling from jail.

"Hello Britton, long time no talk. How's everything going with you?" Range's sleazy voice echoed from the other side of the phone. I didn't say a word as I removed the phone from my face.

"DON'T HANG UP THAT PHONE!" he yelled, causing me to stop breathing. "Put it back up to your ear, Britton!" How in the hell did he know that the phone was away from my ear? Not wanting to piss him off any further, I did as I was told.

"What do you want Range? Now is not a good time."

"I heard that your boy got jammed up." Now I know word travels fast, but not that damn fast. Something was off about this whole encounter.

"I don't know what you're talking about."

"Don't play coy with me, Britton. Word travels fast amongst lawyers. I have some pull around here, and I think I could get those charges dropped."

Even though DJ already had a lawyer, I needed to play the game that Range was setting up for me. He knew a lot more than he was trying to set up, and I was going to find out exactly what he knew by any means necessary.

"Everything comes with a price Range. Name your price."

"You know politics well, Ms. Matthews. Well, since you don't like beating around the bush. In exchange for getting your *friend* released, I would like one weekend with you...alone."

No. Nope. Nah. That wasn't going to happen. Range and I will NEVER be anywhere with just the two of us. He was bat shit crazy if he thought that I was going to go through with this.

"Can I think about?" I needed to stall him as long as possible until I heard from Javi and mama Mack.

"This offer has a shelf life of twenty-four hours, Britton. The clock starts now."

"Wait, you called me private. How am I going to contact you?"

"No need, I'll call you when I feel that you've made up your mind." He hung up the phone without another word.

Without my permission, tears began to fall down my face. This whole situation wasn't sitting with me well with me. I've never given him a hard time during the time that I've known Range. I've just passed on all of his advances. I rested my face in my hands and allowed the tears to flow freely.

"Britton, sweetie, why are you crying?" Mariyah climbed in the seat next to me and wrapped her arms around me. "Stop crying before you bust your stitches. Javi is working diligently to get DJ released. It's going to be fine."

"No mama, it's not. DJ is in there because some bullshit with this guy that won't leave me alone. He wants me and is stopping at nothing to get me. Range knows that DJ is the one for me, and he ain't fuckin' with that. I've gotta stop him ma, but I can't do that while I'm locked in this damn hospital!" I yelled loud enough for the doctors and nurses outside to hear me.

"Aye, young lady, you're gonna need to calm down." Kindred stood at the door with his arms folded across his chest. "You don't need to be out here in these streets in your condition. Javi is good at what she does, and she's gonna take care of him. DJ ain't no weak ass nigga, so him being locked up for a few hours ain't gonna break him. What's gonna break him is if he sees you a broken mess."

As much as I wanted to cut my eyes at him, I had to admit that he was right. I needed to get my act together.

"Thanks, Kindred, I'll get it together." He nodded while taking a seat in the chair next to the door.

"Javi's working her magic with DJ. For now, I need to know everything about Range."

There wasn't much for me to tell. Range and I didn't have *history*. We simply had a few run-ins here and there. He made plenty of advances here and there, but there wasn't enough contact between the two of us that would justify him going crazy.

"There's not much to tell, mama." I broke down our little interactions, but there wasn't much to go on.

"No worries, baby. We're about to meet up with Javi and see what's going on. Sit tight, and I'll be back to check on you." She kissed me on the cheek and slid out of bed. "Hey, have you heard from Ani?"

"No, I haven't heard from her in a little while. DJ has been here with me day in, and day out, so she said she was going to give us some space. I honestly haven't seen her in about four days. That's when she brought me my clothes."

Mariyah pursed her lips at me and then nodded. The two of them exited the room and closed the door behind them.

They could sit back and twiddle their thumbs while waiting on Javi, but I needed information right now, and the only person that would be able to tell me was Range. They couldn't keep me in this hospital against my will. I completely understand the risks of me leaving. However, DJ was more important than all of that.

As I dressed in my clothes, I thought about the first night I was here. Everyone has left, and DJ was the only person allowed to stay in the room. The staff was totally against it. However, he was going to stop at nothing to stay with me.

"What did you have to do in order to stay?" I asked while trying to find a comfortable position to sleep in. Pain rippled through my body with each movement that I made.

"I did what was necessary." He helped me lay down, and he climbed in the bed right behind me. For the next few moments, he just held me. Deep and heavy sighs left his lips, and his hold on me grew tighter. "I can't lose you, Bri."

"I'm not going anywhere. You're stuck with me forever." I let out a chuckle, but quickly stopped when it caused me pain.

"That shit ain't funny, Bri. You got shot twice, ma! On everything I love, I'm going to find out who's responsible."

He was right, this wasn't funny by far, but I use laughter to cope with pain. I'm loud and outspoken so that I don't have to sit in silence and deal with the problems that live within me. I've been doing it for and while, and I'm almost positive that it's going to take a while to move forward.

"I know, baby. I know."

"I'm sorry for spazzin' on you. You wouldn't even be in this position if I hadn't left you."

I really wish people would stop saying that. It wasn't his fault that someone decided to shoot at us. From the looks of it, it was probably unavoidable.

"Baby it's alright. We're going to be fine. I'm going to be fine. I promise."

"I love you, Bri. I wanna make this shit work, and I'm gonna do whatever needs to be done." He began placing soft kisses on my collarbone.

Remembering that night solidified that I was going to do what needed to be done in order to save him. Sleeping with the enemy was never a good thing. I just hope DJ understands that everything I do moving forward is for him. It was time to take matters into my own hands.

As I placed the last of my things in a bag, my cell phone rang. "I'm in."

"Good, someone will be downstairs to pick you up." I could hear his smile through the phone. That right there had me second-guessing my decision, but in order to save DJ, I needed to go through with this.

"I'll need a few things before we go or do anything. Will my driver be able to take me to get them?"

"Absolutely, make sure you pick up something sexy for us. I'll see you soon." It took everything in me not to throw up the contents of my stomach. This was going to be harder than I thought.

41

ANI MACK

For the past few days, I've been hiding out in a hotel room buried knee deep in information. I knew that sooner or later things were going to hit the fan, and I was going to have to hit the ground running. When Owen told me that he believed Camille was the cause of his father's death, I knew that I needed to step in and do something. What's the point of having this power and not using it for the people who held you down? Time and time again, Owen's been there for me, and I'll be damned if I turn my back on him.

Since the night that he came to my house, we've been inseparable. Finally revealing exactly what we mean to each other was more than enough to breathe life into something new. We still had plenty of things to learn about one another, but for now, we had bigger issues to deal with.

"Fuck!" I yelled out in frustration. I had been sitting here for hours trying to find some kind of connection, and I kept hitting dead ends.

"Aye, calm down. You're gonna figure it out," Owen assured me while walking back in the room with a plastic bag in one hand and a drink in the other. He placed them on the bed next to me while opening the blinds and allowing sun rays to penetrate the darkness that I had been in.

"Mmm." The aroma that came from the bag had my attention more than his words. "That smells so good." My mouth started to salivate at the thought of what could be in the bag. At this point, it didn't even matter as long as it was good and edible I didn't even care.

"Take a break and eat. That can wait for a little bit." He set the bag down on the bed, and I quickly grabbed it and began to devour its contents.

"Slow down before you choke." He was laughing at me, but I didn't find anything funny. "Were you able to find anything useful?"

"No, not really," I stated with a mouth full of food. "The only person that I think can really help me is Kindred." I had been doing everything in my power to avoid asking him for help.

"Shit, I was wondering when you would come to your senses." Owen was now seated on the couch with his head in his phone probably playing Toon Blast.

"What's that supposed to mean?"

"You and I both know that you should have gone to him the same damn night. Your pops name holds a lot of weight in these streets. Your name is now out there, but Kin's name is bigger. He's been in the game longer and has more pull than you. You put word out for info, but that well has run dry. I'm almost positive that if *he* put out word, the niggas would have broken their neck to get him what he needed." I hated to admit that he was making a lot of sense. Owen wasn't the typical street guy, but he knew a lot more than he led us to believe.

Against everything that I had been standing for, I reached for my phone and called the number that I hadn't even saved in my phone. The sound of the ringing had me on edge. I had never been so nervous in my life. What if he decided that he didn't want to help me?

"Hello." Hearing his voice on the other end had me stuck.

"H-hey Kindred, do you think that we could meet up? I need your help with a few things." The words spilled out with ease and much faster than I had anticipated.

"Is everything okay? Are you safe? Where are you? We've been worried about you?" He fired off question after question and wasn't allowing me to get a word in. He kept going and going until I was finally fed up.

"Daddy, I'm fine. Calm down!" I yelled into the phone.

Owen's head popped up and our eyes connected. The other end of the phone went silent, and you could hear a pin drop on both ends. The fact that I had called him daddy had everyone stuck. My anxiety was starting to kick in, and to keep it from hitting overdrive, I decided not to acknowledge it.

"Can you just hear me out and help me? Is there someplace where we can meet?"

"Yeah, where are you? I'll come get you."

I gave him my address, and he let me know that he would be here in twenty minutes. That didn't give me much time. I finished my food, kissed Owen, and hopped in the shower.

৯৫৯

WE SAT IN A CAFÉ TUCKED AWAY TRYING TO FIGURE OUT HOW TO start the conversation. There was a time in my life where I prayed for little moments like this. Having a father in my life was something that I longed for since I realized what it meant not to have one. Sitting across the table from him had all kinds of emotions rushing to the forefront. Anger, sadness, happiness, and pain were all there and fighting one another to take the lead.

Before I let one of them win, I opened my mouth to speak.

"Thanks for this. I need some help with finding a connection, and I figure that the start of most of this comes from the long-standing issues between the Edwards and De Lina's."

Kindred stat back in his chair and his eyes turned into slits. He sat like this for about a minute or so before proceeding to give me information that I needed.

"My oldest brother Kendrell had most of the issues with Nikolas. They were business partners, and when greed kicked in, Nik decided that he wanted more."

He continued to tell me everything there was to know about the Edwards and De Lina's. Knowing that Kendrell was a cold-blooded killer and showed little to no mercy had me speechless. That was a bad muthafucka if you ask me.

"Shit," was the only response that I had when he finished talking.

I appreciated the information, and it shed some serious light on who Camille is. In my personal opinion, she suffered from separation anxiety or some shit. She didn't like people she loved being taken away from her. Also, she liked the gutter type bad boy. She and Owen weren't in the same tax bracket when they met. And how she found him was the least of my concern.

"I appreciate you taking the time to help me out. All of this is weird at times, and I don't always know if I'm doing the right thing."

"No problem. This shit isn't easy baby girl, but you have *my* blood flowing through your veins. You're a fighter, and you're not going to let anyone get in the way of what you got going on. You're out here makin' me proud. Don't stop."

"Now that you're out, are you going to come back and take over everything?" He brought his hand to his beard and began stroking it.

"Do you want me to?"

"I want you to do whatever you think is best." His eyes turned into thin slits as he sat deep in thought.

"Then it's yours. Your mother wouldn't allow me back in the game as the head even if I wanted to. Mariyah is a stubborn ass woman." He had that right. She didn't play when it came to the people that she loved. She lost him once, and I'm positive that she's not gonna lose him again. "Do you have plans for the business?

"My first order of business right now is to kill Camille De Lina. We have reason to believe that she killed Owen's father, and she's the one that shot up the bar. Her actions are inexcusable, and she needs to be handled accordingly. There's one more thing that I need to do before I head down that road."

"Damn, you look like Kendrell. I don't care how you go about this. It seems as though you know what you're doing, but I want you to be careful. If you need any help, don't hesitate to ask."

"I got it," was all I said. In response, he nodded and accepted my words. "Can we do this again? Just hang out and um, get to know each other." His eyes lit up with shock, and it slightly warmed my heart.

"Definitely."

42

ANI MACK

Talking to Kindred had shed so much light on the current situation. However, not all of my questions about Camille were answered. What better person was there out there to answer them other than her father? Nikolas knew why his daughter was the way she was. I was determined to know everything about her, and I was going to get answers one way or another.

"I'm coming with you," Owen stated as I threw clothes into a duffle bag.

"No, you're not. This is something that I have to do for myself."

"Ani, this is bullshit. You can't travel to another city with no protection. You're asking to get hurt. You're stepping into *their* territory. If the crazy bitch got people trying you in *your* territory, then why the fuck would you go into the lion's den?"

"Trust me," was all I said as I grabbed the duffle bag and walked to the front door.

During my drive to the airport, I thought of all the different ways this could go wrong. I was prepared for things to go south. Hopefully, I'll be able to get what I need and get back home without incident.

As the plane prepared for departure, I texted Britton and told her that I loved her. She had been a little MIA lately, but I was too. We tended to do these things when we had stuff going on, yet we'd be right back to one another when we were finished.

๑๑๑

As I drove from LAX, I allowed the LA sun to shine down on me. On the outside, I may have looked calm cool and collected. However, on the inside, a storm was brewing, and I was ready for war. Camille had caused too much pain to this family, and I wasn't having it anymore. After checking into my hotel and getting settled, I drove to the city of Calabasas. I reached a gated home and had to double check to see if I had the correct address for Nik. The home was nice, modest beachfront home, but it definitely wasn't what I expected out of a "cartel boss". It was modest, to say the least.

The gate buzzed, and a voice called out over the speaker. *"Miss, you have the wrong address. Please turn around and exit the property."* I pressed the buzzer again and again until some answered me.

"I'm here to see Nikolas De Lina. Please tell him that Ani *Edwards* is here to see him. Thanks."

As soon as I said my last name, the gate began to open. When I pulled into the driveway, two armed guards stood in front of the double doors along with who I can only assume was Nikolas. He was a short, older Hispanic man with a decent amount of swag.

My six-inch heels hit the pavement as I exited the car. I straightened out the fitted pants suit that I was rocking and flipped my long hair behind my back. The guards gripped their guns tighter with every step that I took.

"Good evening, Nikolas. I'm Ani." I reached my hand out to shake his, and two semi-automatic weapons were pointed directly at my face. This would have scared the hell out of me a few months ago, but after being shot at on multiple occasions, it started to bother me less and less. If they thought that I was any threat to Nik, they would have blasted my car before the gates closed.

"Good evening, Ani. And to what do I owe this visit?" he asked while puffing on a cigar.

"I'm sure you know why I'm here. All girls call their father when they're in trouble." I smirked at him, and he nodded in return.

"Come in. Let's chat."

❧ 43 ❧

BRITTON MATTHEWS

My palms were saturated with sweat as I handed the attendant my boarding pass. I had no business getting on this plane and going to New York. Before Range gave me my flight details, Javi left me a voicemail saying that they were going to hold him as long as they could, and they were hitting him with serious drug charges. She was working diligently. However, it wasn't quick enough. Playing Range's game was going to get this situation put behind us.

My phone vibrated in my hand while I walked to my seat. Ani had sent a text telling me that she loved me. It was odd because we hadn't spoken to each other in days. I started to respond, but then I decided against it. If I responded to her, then I was going to have the urge to tell her the stupid shit I had gotten myself into.

As I settled in my seat, the pain from my wounds was starting to get to me. Getting out of the hospital was hell, but after a few f-bombs and threats of lawsuits, they were more than happy to get me out of their hair. They were right in trying to keep me. It was far too early for me to be moving around let alone taking a two-hour flight to New York.

Damn Britton, what have you gotten yourself into? This question played over and over in my head as the plane prepared for takeoff. I stopped the flight attendant for some water and swallowed two pain pills. I didn't have plans on staying in New York for too long. Range was going to give me what I needed one way or another.

❧

"MA'AM, WE'VE ARRIVED," THE FLIGHT ATTENDANCE LIGHTLY TAPPED my shoulder. I thanked her and grabbed my things.

Range was sending someone to pick me up. I didn't trust it, so I placed glasses over my eyes and made my way to a car rental counter. He believed that he was going to run things and I was going to be on his time. In all honesty, I had the upper hand, and he was going to soon realize that.

The ringing of my phone startled me as I made my way to Manhattan. "Hello," I answered as sweetly as possible.

"You don't follow directions, Britton. Your flight landed approximately thirty minutes ago. Why aren't you with the driver?"

"Because I'm grown as fuck and do what I want to do. Look, I'm here, and that's all that matters. Dinner is at seven, and I'll be there dressed to impress. Until then, leave me be and let me get my head on straight. Bye!" I hung up the phone and tossed it in the driver's seat.

❧

AS I GAVE MYSELF THE ONCE OVER IN THE FLOOR LENGTH MIRROR, I noticed that the time on the clock read *6:50 p.m.* I was moving at a leisurely pace, and it was just enough to tick Range off. One thing that I knew about him was that he loathed tardiness. The restaurant was at least a twenty-minute drive from the hotel. It was in my plans to tap dance on his last nerve and then do what needed to be done.

Stepping on the elevator, I held my clutch purse close to my body along with my black overnight bag. This night needed to go the way that I had planned it. A part of me wanted to turn around, forget all of this, and take my chances with Javi. Unfortunately, that would take up too much time and money. I finally got myself together and strutted my ass to the car.

"DJ you better be lucky that I love you!" I shouted at the top of my lungs while turning up the music and speeding off into the night.

When I arrived at the restaurant, I was at least twenty minutes late. Range had sent a massive amount of text messages informing me that he wasn't happy. He was right where I needed him to be. As I walked through the restaurant behind the hostess, all eyes were on me. The dress was mesmerizing and paired with my body. It was going to break a few necks.

The hostess opened the door to the private room and introduced me. His mouth fell to the floor when his eyes fell on me. I had a silver sparkling mini dress that did not pass the "fingertip test". My blonde hair was nice and curly while my makeup was done to perfection.

"Good evening, Mr. St. John." I thanked the hostess for her help and proceeded to sit at the table across from him.

"W-wow," was all he was able to muster up.

"Let's get this dinner over with so that we can get to the good stuff." I hit him with a wink and blew him a kiss.

An hour and a half later, we were finished with dinner, and I was back at his hotel. I knew what was next for us, and I prayed to the high heavens that things wouldn't get *that* far.

"Brit, you almost done?" he said while entering the bathroom.

I was currently taking an extended shower while also downing a glass of D'usse. If I was going to do this, then alcohol was absolutely necessary.

"I'll be out there when I'm good and got damn ready! Close the door and let me finish getting my shit together!" I chugged the contents of the glass and sent it flying towards the door. Range coward behind the door and slammed it shut without another word.

I finally exited the shower and put on the little outfit that I brought along with me. Range was going to remember this weekend for the rest of his life. One thing I don't take well to is authority. I only fear a few people on God's green earth, and Range is not one of them. The liquor was giving me all the courage that I needed right now. I reached for my glass then realized that I had smashed it. Placing the bottle at my lips, I chugged what was left and wiped my mouth clean with the back of my hand.

"Britton baby, are you ready?" Range called out.

"Yes daddy, are *you* ready for me?" I had to close my mouth to keep from gagging.

Before I exited the bathroom, I checked my outfit one last time in the mirror. The black dominatrix outfit fit my short thick frame perfectly. The thigh-high leather boots were overkill, but I needed to sell this shit as best as I could.

When I opened the bathroom door, I grabbed my black bag and walked out. Range was sprawled out on the bed with only a pair of black boxers on. His arms were resting behind his head while his eyes faced the ceiling. He had yet to realize that I was in the room. In order to get his attention, I tossed the bag to the side, and his head turned in my direction. The moment he saw what I was wearing, his eyes damn near popped out of his head.

"You ready to play a game?" His eyes lit up, and everything was going just the way I had hoped.

44

KINDRED EDWARDS

Ani was about to go do some rogue shit, and I needed to get there before she did something she would regret. She moved pretty quickly after I dropped her off this afternoon. Fire danced in her eyes as she told me why she believed that Camille was the cause for all of this. She reminded me so much of Kendrell and myself, and if I knew her like I thought I did, she was going to the source of all the commotion.

I packed a bag as quickly as I could before Riyah made it back home. I grabbed a duffle and threw in what I could. Thankfully, I was able to get in and get out before she made it back. If she knew what was going on, she was going to hop her ass in the car and demand to come along with me. My only reason for going to Nik's house was to make sure that he didn't try anything with Ani. Other than that, I was going to sit back and let her handle this shit on her own.

After I arrived in LA, I went straight to Nik's house. Ani wasn't there so she must have made an additional stop. When I pulled up to the gate, I pressed the buzzer and waited for security to talk. This wasn't my first time at Nik's house. However, the last time I was here, the conversation was on less than friendly terms.

"What you want?" he yelled over the phone.

"Gabe, open the fuckin' gate. Nik and I need to have a few words."
He let out a deep sigh while the gate opened in front of me. I sped into
the driveway, parked and hopped out.

"Man, why do you always come in here talkin' big shit to me?
Punkin' me in front of my team."

"Shit your team already knows you're a punk. They didn't need my
help with that." I walked up to Niko and slapped hands with him.
Gabe and I were like Ken and Nik before the fallout. Even though
they fell out, we didn't. We kept shit civil and respected each other's
boundaries.

"Aye, man watch yaself, but Nik is in the crib. Gone 'head in."

"Shit, we've kept our part of the treaty, so the reason behind this
visit is beyond me. What can I help you with Kindred?" Nikolas came
into the living room area where I was seated.

"Have a seat we need to rap about a few things."

"If this has anything to do with my daughter and your daughter,
please know that I had nothing to do with any of this. Camille is—"

"Camille is Gloriana's daughter. She acts just like her." I couldn't
help but chuckle. "She's stubborn and strongwilled. She doesn't give up
easily when it's something that she wants." A smile formed on his face
as he thought about Gloriana.

We continued to talk for a few minutes before Gabe was yelling
over the intercom system.

"Aye, that's Ani she's coming to talk to you on some real shit, Nik.
Listen to her and answer her questions. You know how I get down so
don't fuck this up. Don't tell her I'm here." He nodded and went back
to puffin' on the cigar, and I got up and walked into the adjacent room
to listen.

"Good evening, Ani. And to what do I owe this visit?" his voice was
a little shaky. If he was going to do this, then he needed to get his shit
under control.

"I'm sure you know why I'm here. All girls call their father when
they're in trouble."

"Come in. Let's chat."

45

ANI MACK

Nikolas and I were sitting across from one another engaged in an intense staredown. He knew exactly why I was here and waiting for me to get to the point. Camille was wreaking havoc in my life, and it was time to put an end to it.

"I know why you're here," he said while sipping the liquid in his glass.

"I'm going to kill your daughter, plain and simple." The words left my mouth, and he didn't flinch one bit.

"What makes you think that I'm going to allow that to happen?" He still hadn't moved, and it was evident to me that this wasn't going to be as much of a blow to him as I thought.

"From your lack of a reaction, it seems as though you're just as tired of your daughter as I am." He finally moved, and it was only to relax a little in his seat.

"Cami has separation anxiety. Ever since her mother was killed—"

"By you."

"You do your homework. That's good. But yes, ever since I killed her mother, Camille has done any and everything to hold onto the people that she's closest with. If she loves you, she'll dig her claws into you, and it's going to be hard as hell to shake her. In the beginning, she comes off as a loving and friendly person. A few months into the situation, she turns into a controlling and dramatic ass person. Who wants to deal with that all the time?"

"Why didn't you get her help? For a big-time, player like you, a therapist shouldn't cost too much."

"Shit, she went through therapists like people change drawers. It didn't work, and after a while, I gave up."

"What kind of father gives up on their child?"

"Is that a path that *you* really want to go down and talk about?" He hit me with a wink and a smirk, and before he could register, I had two guns pointed at him, one at his head and the other at his heart.

"Don't make me pull the trigger. I have no problem spilling your brains out on this nice ass Persian rug."

"You are truly Kindred's daughter. Put the gun down. There's no need for that. We can keep things civil. Let's discuss the matter at hand. Why do you think that I'll give you my blessing to kill my first and only child?"

"Let's get one thing straight. I'm not here to *ask* for permission or a blessing. I'm going to do what needs to be done regardless. I figured it was best to let you know my reasoning behind what I'm about to do. You can do with it what you will. However, just know that my reach is very long, and if you want to start a war, then we can take it there. Our families have had peace for quite some time, so I hope that we can keep this streak going." I politely tucked my guns behind my back and stood to leave. "Now, before I leave, I need to know the connection between Camille and a man named Esteban. What can you tell me about them?"

"Esteban is an up and coming hustler out in the Santa Ana area. He's been in love with Camille and this business since his younger days. He's been working hard to get on my team, but I didn't allow it. I run a family business, and he's not a part of la familia.

A little while ago, Camille and Esteban ran into each other when she came here on an unexpected trip. If I had to put my detective hat on, she got her claws into him and promised him something other than death. What makes you ask?"

"Well, that's just one of the reasons why I plan on killing her. She had her boy toy come to *my* city and shoot at my girls and me. My best friend got hit twice and will never be the same. Physically she'll be fine, but mentally..." I expressed while tapping my own forehead. "...mentally, she'll never be the same, and that's inexcusable. And let's not get me started on how she killed her boyfriend's father."

His eyes grew wide at that revelation. Uneasiness filled his face and a tear welled in his left eye. I was trained on his reaction to see if he had known any of this. By the shaking of his hand, he didn't know how foul his daughter was living.

"Ani," he cleared his throat and took whatever was in his glass to the head. "Do what needs to be done."

I stood from the couch and began walking towards the door. Nothing more needed to be said. It was time to go back home and do what needed to be done. As I placed my hand on the knob, a familiar voice was behind me.

"You're a smart man, Nik."

I'm not sure how Kindred made it here before me nor did I know why he was here, but to know that he let me do my own thing brought a sinister smile to my face. I was finally handling things like a cartel boss. With a smile on my face, I strutted down the stairs and got in my car. Goodbye LA, I hope to never see you again.

❧ 46 ❧

BRITTON MATTHEWS

"**A**re you ready to play a game?" I asked Range one last time before I got started.

"Hell yeah, baby, I'm ready for anything. I knew you wanted me just as much as I wanted you—"

"Shut up! It's not your time to talk. I'll let you know when you can speak." He flexed his jaw but kept his mouth closed.

"Stand up, right now." He did.

"Now sit down." He quickly sat down, but not before attempting to open his mouth. "Don't make me say it again." Instead of talking, he nodded and kept his eyes trained on me.

"From this point on, I'm in charge. You will listen to everything I say, and you will follow my directions to a tee. If not, you will be punished. Do you understand?"

His eyes looked as though they were going to pop out of his head. Range wasn't used to having someone tell him what to do. From the look on his face and his lip being slightly tucked into his mouth, he was loving all of this. For the next twenty minutes, Range was a slave to my words and actions. He was much more obedient than I anticipated.

The games that I was playing with him were only going to last so long. His attention span was running low, and if I wanted to get DJ freed, I needed to dig into him right now. While he was cuffed to the bed with a blindfold, I popped two pain pills in my mouth and gulped them down dry. That was possibly the worst decision I've ever made because it caused me to start coughing.

"Britton, is everything okay?" he asked while trying to free his arms from the handcuffs.

"Y-yes now lay back." I finally got my breaths under control and proceeded to grab a few items out of my bag.

"You've been so good to me tonight Range, and I want to continue what we have going on. If you're up for it, I want to take the kinky up a notch. What we've been doing is fine and all, but I want to know how far you'll go. Are you okay with that?"

"I'm fine with anything you do. None of it will leave this room. Damn, I can't wait to be inside of you." Hearing him say that almost made me throw up the contents of my stomach.

With my feather whip, I traced along his abs and then smacked them a few times. He winced from the pain and then a smile formed on his face. I climbed on the bed and straddled him.

"Why was Dorian Cruttwell arrested?" I asked while moving my hips back and forth against the growing bulge in his boxers.

"T-they had reason to believe that he was in possession of a controlled substance. Damn girl, why can't you just put it in already?" Instead of smacking him with the whip, I used a different kind of toy on him.

"I didn't ask for additional comments. Stick to answering questions, not asking them!" he yelled out in pain as I pressed my seal knife into him breaking his skin in two and allowing the blood to seep through.

"Now, tell me if he actually had anything on him."

"N-no. He didn't."

"So, you're comfortable putting away an innocent black man? For what, Range? For me? Now that's just stupid. I know I'm cute and all with a fat ass, but baby, I'm crazy, and I come with a lot of problems. You should have gotten to know me before you did all of that."

There were now multiple lines across his chest from where the knife connected to his skin.

"I just had to have you, Britton. He was getting in the way of that, and I'm sorry! If you stop, I'll make a call to the DA's office and have the charges dropped. He owes me a favor. Just please stop hitting me!" he cried out in agony.

This was much easier than I thought. Range could walk around town like a tough guy all he wanted, but he was nothing more than a coward in a suit. I hopped off him quickly and scanned his pants pockets for the phone.

"Whose name do I need to call?" He was focused on his pain and not me. "Focus, Range!"

"Ahh, Rosenburg. Look for Martin Rosenburg."

"Before I press send on this phone, there needs to be some ground rules set. If you mention anything other than releasing Dorian, then we're going to have bigger problems than me piercing your skin with my knife. If you fuck this up in any way...so help me God, I will make your life a living hell. Do you understand me?"

"Y-yeah, I got it."

I placed the call to the DA, and the two of them shared a few words with one another. From the sounds of it, the DA was buying everything Range was selling. By the end of the conversation, DJ was going to be released within the hour. My time here in New York wasn't in vain, and I just hope that DJ understood why I did this. From the outside looking in, one would think that I was betraying the man that I loved. However, I was really doing what needed to be done to secure his freedom.

"If you ever step near anyone that I'm associated with, I want you to remember this day. Remember what I am capable of, and know that I am not one to play with when it comes to my people. Now I'm gonna put this in your mouth because what's about to happen next is gonna hurt like hell."

I stuffed a washcloth in his mouth and then grabbed a bottle of rubbing alcohol from my bag. When he saw the alcohol, he began squirming on the bed like a roach that had just been sprayed with raid.

"This might sting a little...or a lot. Think if this like cleaning a big ass paper cut."

Pouring the liquid onto his chest, I watched as he begged for mercy. I'm usually the fun and loving type, but when someone messes over my family, the gloves come off, and there's no limit to what I can do.

"Now I'm going to release you from these cuffs once I finish getting dressed. If you even think about calling the cops just know that our whole encounter has been filmed. What would the city say when they found out that their best lawyer likes getting spa—"

"Okay!" he yelled while spitting the washcloth out of his mouth. "I get it. You don't have to blackmail me. I'm already humiliated enough."

"Then my work here is done."

❦ 47 ❦

MARIYAH MACK

Ani and Kindred thought they were slick. They both slipped out of this city to visit Nikolas thinking that I wouldn't find out. I'm the queen when it comes to finding things out. Hopefully, they found the answers they were looking for and didn't start a damn war with the De Lina's.

Things were a mess around here. I had Ani and Kindred sneaking off to LA thinking that I wouldn't find out. Britton had checked herself out of the hospital and was missing in action. I also had Javi working overtime to get DJ released from jail. My family was determined to put me into the looney bin.

"Javi, tell me you've got good news."

Javi had called while I was headed home after a long day of running errands. When she explained to me that DJ had been released along with all of his charges being dropped, my heart jumped for joy. She was good at what she did, and that's why she made the big bucks. At least that's what I had originally thought until she told me that the DA called and personally told the police to release him. I don't know how it was done nor do I care to know. Some things are better left unsaid.

As soon as we hung up, I tried calling Britton to tell her the good news. However, her phone kept going to voicemail. I just pray that she's alright and not laying in a ditch somewhere. Lord knows we don't need any more bloodshed.

I had just hung up from trying to contact Britton when my phone rang. "Hello," I answered. It was an unknown number, and normally, I wouldn't have answered. However, with my family not within arm's reach, it could have been important.

"Mariyah Mack, is this you?" a young lady's voice came out of the receiver. I'd never heard this voice before.

"Yes, this is she. How can I help you?"

"I hope you're wearing your seatbelt."

Before I could register what was said to me, a car flashed their bright lights directly in front of me causing me to veer out of its path. My sudden move of the steering wheel caused my car to turn on its side and roll until it rested upside down.

Broken glass was everywhere, and blood trickled down my face. It hurt to move my body, and I'm almost positive that I may have broken something. I tried to move, but the seatbelt had activated, and I was locked in.

Hearing someone stepping on broken glass had my nerves on high. It dawned on me that what happened wasn't an accident. Someone was trying to kill me. It was probably the same person that tried to kill Ani, Britton, and Skylar. I sent up a prayer and asked God to help me escape this nightmare before I closed my eyes to play dead.

"Is she dead?" I could hear the same voice that was just on my phone.

"I'm not sure, shorty. Check her pulse." If they checked my pulse, then I was as good as dead.

"I'm not touching a dead body, Esteban."

Esteban? Why did that name sound so familiar?

"Fuck it Cami. She hasn't moved to escape the car, so she's dead. Let's just get the hell out of here before the cops come. I can't believe you've dragged me into your bullshit."

Cami? Oh shit, that's Owen's girlfriend's name.

I heard the car doors slam shut and the engine purred before they sped off into the night. In my attempt to ensure that they were gone, I waited a few minutes before slipping through my seatbelt and falling forward on to the windshield. This car was good and totaled, but that was the least of my worries. This shit could be replaced at the snap of my fingers.

My driver's side window was still intact, but the door wasn't opening. The only way for me to get out was to kick the damn thing in. My body was tired at this point, and if I didn't hurry, I was going to die on this back road.

"Fight, Riyah. You got this."

Trying to give yourself a pep talk while in pain is probably one of the hardest things to do. At this point, it was now or never— mind over matter. I dug my heels into that window and pushed with everything I had. It finally came crashing down, allowing me to slide out. A car pulled up alongside me, and the driver got out. I had never been so scared in my life before. The darkness of the night didn't allow me to see their face, and I just knew it was Camille coming to finish the job.

"Riyah? Is that you?" I could hear Tony's voice, but I couldn't see him. My eyes had closed, and my body hit the pavement like a sack of potatoes.

⚜️

"I'M SO TIRED OF SEEING YOUR FAMILY IN AND OUT OF THIS DAMN hospital. I'm pleading the blood of Jesus over all of y'all." The sounds of someone fussing caused my eyes to flutter open and then quickly shut due to the extremely bright light.

"And we're tired of seeing you too," Britton mumbled under her breath. I wanted to laugh at her childishness, but the pain was too severe.

"I heard that, little girl. In a minute, I'm going to have them hold a room for you guys for when one of you gets hurt. Shootings, car crashes, murder? What in God's name are you into?"

"Drugs old lady, we're into drugs," Britton spoke out once again while causing the doctor to gasp at her bluntness. I could hear Ani snickering in the background.

"Dr. Young, I would like to apologize for Britton's behavior. She's still not over the other people trying to hold her hostage."

"Mmhmm, well Ms. Mack is doing well today. It's only been about a day. There hasn't been any change in her condition. However, it's not due to any brain damage. Her body has physically shut down in order to recharge itself. She'll be good to go a few days after her body wakes up."

"I'm up." I finally opened my eyes and spoke up. All of the eyes in the room were now focused on me. One by one, they rushed over to me to see if I was okay.

"Mommy, what the hell happened?"

"Camille."

48

ANI MACK

C amille was making moves, and I'd allowed her to breathe too long. Killing Owen's father, Britton being shot twice, and my mother getting in a car accident was too much to let slip through the cracks. She was well overdue for getting her ass handed to her.

"You ready for this?" Owen asked as I paced back and forth in my bedroom.

"I stay ready."

"What's your plan? How are you going to go about this? You can't go into this shit with no plan. That's the easiest way to get killed."

"Okay, since you know so much about her. How do you suppose I go about this?"

"Easy. You have me."

Owen was seated on the sofa in my room cutting away at an apple. If he thought for one second that I was going to use him to get to Camille...then he was right. He pulled his phone out and sat it on the table.

"That's not a bad idea. She hasn't directly targeted you because she's still in love with you and thinks that she has a chance. She doesn't have a chance...does she?"

A. GAVIN

He set the knife and apple on the table and got up from the couch.

"You tell me. Do you think she does?" he asked while moving my hoodie to the side unzip my hoodie. He followed the zipped down while placing a gentle and warm kiss on that area of exposed skin. The feeling of his lips on me was taking me to a new height. With each kiss, I could feel the love he had for me traveling through my body.

With my hoodie fully unzipped and exposing my breasts, he stood to his feet and his body towered over mine. His face showed passion and fire as he studied every inch of me. His eyes tore through me, and I was burning from within. I wanted nothing more than to have him right now. I found myself biting my lip while thinking of all the things that I wanted to do to him.

"Don't bite your bottom lip."

Being disobedient, I bit my lip again and watched as his thick tongue glided against his smooth lips. He lifted his arms and pulled his t-shirt over his head. His golden skin glistened against the slivers of moonlight that came through the blinds.

He tossed the shirt to the side while I grabbed his waist and brought him back down to the bed. "I need to feel you...now."

"Your wish is my command."

His head made its way past my breasts and down to my navel. I gasped when he reached the top of my pants and unbuttoned them with his teeth. Soft moans continuously escaped my lips as Owen worked his magic.

"Hello? Helllooooo! Owen is that you?"

"Yes Owen, right there!" I yelled out completely disregarding the fact that Camille was on the other end of the phone listening.

THE NEXT NIGHT

After Owen set the trap with Camille, she had been blowing up his phone nonstop. At this point, she was desperate to get in contact with him. She went from begging him to come home and talk to her to telling him that he needed to come and get his things. This is exactly the reaction that I wanted from her. She was going to lose her mind slowly but surely.

"What are you over there thinking about?" Owen and I were by the lakefront enjoying the night air while stargazing, one of the most relaxing things I've done since I took on this position. From the moment I saw Kindred at the courthouse, my life has been a nonstop rollercoaster.

"Finally gaining some peace." With Nolton gone and Camille next, I looked forward to actually doing what needed to be done for this company.

"I feel you on that. Shit's been really crazy around here, and you've held your own, Ani. I'm proud of you shorty." I was seated in between his legs while he had his arms wrapped around me. I turned my head up to look at him, and I was met with his lips crashing into mine.

"I love you, Owen," I said in between kisses.

"I love—" Before he was able to finish his sentence, his phone rang for the third time in less than five minutes.

"Just answer it. I'm ready to get this shit over with." The mood was ruined, and I was more than ready to pay Ms. De Lina a visit.

Owen was obviously just as frustrated as I was. "Hello?" he answered with more bass in his voice than normal.

"Come get your shit right now, Owen! Right now, or I will burn it ALLLL!" He nodded, and that was my cue to get ready for the deed to be done.

"I'll be there when I get there. You don't run shit. Do you understand me?" he roared into the phone. This was the loudest that he's ever been around me. Owen kept true to the cool calm and collected persona.

"I-I'm sorry. I just want you to come home so that we can talk about this. I want you to know that I forgive you for everything. I'm sure the little slut seduced you into doing those things. Owen, she's no good for you. Do you know what she does for a living?"

My ears perked up at that moment. There was no telling who might have been listening to this phone conversation. Owen must have noticed the shift in my body language.

"Aye, I'll be there tonight. We can talk about all of this then."

"Okay baby, I'll see you soon," she cooed into the phone.

Camille's attitude had done a one-eighty when he mentioned that he would be there tonight. She was missing more than a few loose screws. But that's okay, I planned on fixing that problem real soon.

No words were said as Owen and I headed back to the car. It was time to finish what we started and move on with our lives. We'd been playing games with people for too long.

49

BRITTON MATTHEWS

"What's the word?" I answered groggily into the phone. It was only 9:30 p.m., but I was damn near out like a light.

"It's time. You ready?" Ani asked on the other end of the phone. I quickly jumped up to get out of the bed. Only to be pulled down by a strong pair of arms. DJ grabbed hold of my face and looked into my eyes.

"Bring your ass back to me in one-piece, Britton. Do you understand me?"

I nodded my head as best as I could since he had a death grip on my jaws. I understood his protectiveness at this point. The man loved me more than the air that he breathed. He was going to do everything in his power to keep me safe and never put me in a position to get hurt.

The day that he was released from jail, I was nowhere to be found and caused panic to spread throughout the family. They didn't know that I was still in New York waiting to get back to the city. DJ blew up my phone nonstop, but I found myself being unable to pick it up and talk to him. Everything that I had just done for him was still weighing heavy on my mind. To think that I risked my life to save this man proved to me that I loved him from the depths of my soul.

The moment that my foot touched Chicago soil, DJ was right there waiting on me. I couldn't even make it off the plane before I was getting snatched up and dragged to the parking garage. How this fool made it past security, I would never know.

"Wait baby slow down. Let me explain!" I pleaded to him.

"What you gotta explain, Bri? That you're a cheating ass female that couldn't even hold a nigga down for twenty-four-hours? I was only in that bitch for twenty-four hours! Damn!" I snatched my arm out of his hand and brought my head to the back of his head.

"Now wait a got damn minute! What you aren't about to do is sit here start making assumptions for shit you don't know about! Ask me why the fuck I was in New York DJ. Go ahead and ask me!"

We were now in the parking garage having a shouting match. My flight landed the next evening since that was the earliest flight I could get out. People were staring at us as they made their way to their cars.

"Fuck y'all lookin' at? Y'all ain't ever had a disagreement with someone? I ain't smacked her ass so keep it moving, nosey ass bitches."

"DJ! Get in the damn car, and I'll explain what happened." I placed my hand on the door handle to open it, but it was still locked. "Open the door."

"Nah, ride on the hood. I don't fuck with op ass bit—"

"Finish that sentence and so help me God I'm going to slap fire from you. Open this fuckin' door before I cause a damn scene. You know I'm good for it. Remember Summer '16 in Philly?" His eyes grew wide at the thought of us being handcuffed together in the back of a squad car in Philly. That night we were arguing heavy, and I smashed his windshield to a million pieces. "Exactly, now get in the car so that I can tell you what happened."

"Stop playin' with me, Bri. I'm not that punk ass nigga Range," he said while unlocking the doors and getting in.

During the ride home, I explained EVERYTHING to him, and by the time I was done, his mouth was wide open. I even went as far as to show him pictures of the damage I'd done. There was only one copy of the SD drive, and I planned on giving it to DJ. He could do what he wanted to do with them. I just needed him to know that those pictures ensured his safety from here on out.

For the remainder of our drive home, he kept quiet. His eyes were focused on the road as he twirled the small chip through his fingers. One could only assume what was going on through his head. When the time was right, he would tell me what was on his mind.

"I'll be fine. I promise. I'll be back before the sun comes up." I kissed his forehead and threw on my clothes.

I jumped in my car and sped to the address Ani sent to me. Thankfully, it was only ten or so minutes from DJ's condo downtown. Ani instructed me to park a few streets over and then meet her at the black van parked across the street by the corner store. I followed the instructions and knocked on the back of the van door three times.

"Open up, bitch. Let's get this show on the road!" I whispered loud enough for her to hear. The back of the door swung open, and I was quickly pulled in. It caught me by surprise and damn near caused me to have whiplash.

"Wait a minute now, lil mama. You didn't have to pull me in like that. I almost thought that I had the wrong van."

"My bad, Brit. I just couldn't take the chance of you being seen," she explained while we settled in. "Owen is inside right now *gathering* his things. It shouldn't be too long before we swoop in and do what needs to be done."

Ani had come up with a plan to kidnap Camille, take her to the warehouse, and do the deed there. To me, it sounded like a lot of work, but this was her show to run.

"Aye, isn't that Esteban?"

I remembered his face from the night of the shooting. I couldn't forget it even if I wanted to. He was tiptoeing from the side of the building trying to get away. If I had to guess, he was in the apartment when Owen showed up, and Camille snuck him out somehow. The broad was dirty no matter how you flipped it.

"Yeah, that's him. You wanna grab him too?"

"Hell yeah, paybacks a bitch, and I'm that bitch today!"

I quickly jumped out of the car and patted my back to make sure that I was strapped. Esteban thought that he was in the clear once he got out of the apartment building. He leaned against the side of the building and fidgeted a little. His back was to me, and it was the perfect opportunity to catch him slipping.

"If you move, I'm gonna blow your head off your shoulders." He damn near jumped out of his skin when he felt the cold steel pressed against his flesh. "You're gonna walk with me over to that van like we're the happiest couple alive. Do you understand me?"

"Y-yeah man I got you," he said while we walked to the car arm in arm. "Who the fuck are you, and why are you messin' with me?"

"I promise all of your questions will be answered in just a second," I voiced while just before the van doors opened up.

"Do you remember me, Esteban?" Ani asked before smiling and punching him in the face and knocking him out cold. We got him into the van and tied up before our next victim would be making their appearance.

50

ANI MACK

Owen and Camille were taking too long for my liking. If they weren't out within the next five minutes, then I was going to go in the apartmeont and drag her out by the hair on her head. My patience was growing thinner by the minute, and soon, I was going to explode.

"Calm down, Ani. I can see your jaw flexing. It's going to go the way we planned." Brit was trying her best to keep me calm, but nothing was working. The only thing that was going to calm me down was having my eyes on Camille and seeing her suffer at my hands. "Wait, look at the door. Something's happening."

Owen pushed the front door open, and Camille was right on his heels. She was dressed in a sexy negligée, and I can only imagine what the hell was going on. Tears streamed down her face as she tugged and pulled on his arm trying to get him to go back into the building. If this was going to go the way, we planned then Owen needed to not draw any unnecessary attention to them.

"Come on, Owen. Get her to shut up."

No sooner than the words left my mouth, he wrapped his arm around her waist and brought her close to him. It seems as though he whispered something in her ear, and it got her to calm down. Without force, the two of them walked together to the van, and she climbed in the back without force. What the hell did he say to her that got her to do this willingly? I decided not to ask the question as I jumped in the driver's seat and Owen climbed in the passenger side. Britton saw the whole thing taking place as well, but she too kept her mouth shut about the whole ordeal.

The drive to the warehouse was quiet. Everyone but Esteban, was in their own thoughts, he was simply sleeping. For me, I wonder what's next for me. Was this what my life was going to be like? Was I going to fight someone off every other day when it came to this damn job? What was I to do next? Give it all away and go back to being normal or moving forward and actually tackling the challenges presented to me. I had a big decision to make, and it wasn't going to be an easy one.

As I pulled the car up to the back of the warehouse, I brushed all of those thoughts to the side. The only thing that I wanted on my mind right now was getting rid of the biggest problem in my family's lives. They didn't deserve to be shot at, killed, and even have their cars run off the road. If Camille would have been an adult about this then maybe, we could have gotten somewhere with all of this. From what I've learned, this game is grimy, and sometimes you just have to step out of your comfort zone and do what needs to be done.

Owen touched my arm before I stepped out of the van. He looked at me and studied my eyes for a brief moment. Fire and ice were dancing throughout my body, and I'm sure it resonated on my face. I was ready for this moment. I was more than ready to free the beast that had been growing deep inside of my soul. It was time for Ani the cartel boss to transform and be everything that she needed to be.

As instructed, my crew placed Esteban and Camille in the chairs with their arms and legs bound together. They couldn't move even if they wanted to.

"Why are you doing this?" Camille had the nerve to ask as I took a seat on the table in front of them.

"You really have no idea why all of this is happening? Is it really not registering to you right now? Even with Esteban sitting next to you?"

Damn, this broad was dumber than I thought. A blank stare graced her face as she tried to think about why she was here.

"Killing Mr. Henry? Having Esteban shoot at my girls and me? Really? None of this is coming back to you?"

"I-I was just trying to save my relationship. You were taking Owen from me, and I couldn't let you have him?" She sobbed as tears streamed down her face. This was comical and downright stupid.

"Seriously, what made you kill his father? Out of all the things you could have done, you took the only person that the *love of your life* had."

"It's clear that Henry didn't like me, and he would have never accepted our relationship moving forward. How could I get my happily ever after if he didn't want his son to be with me?" Tears streamed down her face and it was absolutely unbelievable.

"Camile, I was going to draw this out and cause you all kinds of harm and pain. However—"

"My father isn't going to let my death go unnoticed, Ani!" She screamed out as she tried to fight her way out of the restraints. "Killing me will start a war, a war that you will lose!"

"A war that I've already won. Your father agreed to this."

A smile came across my face as I swung my legs back and forth in front of me. When she first heard the words, she didn't think that I was serious. Her eyes went from me to Owen. He was standing by the door with his arms folded like the very first time we were at this warehouse. There was never a time that he wasn't here for me, and I loved him for that more than he knew. He winked at me and nodded his head at Camille. She had no idea about my conversation with Nikolas.

"Can we kill this bitch already? My man is waiting for me at home, and if I'm late getting back to him, he's gonna bring his black ass in here and fuck us all up. So, can we please move this along?" Britton walked into the room causing the crew to laugh.

"You got it, Britt! You wanna do the honors of this one right here?" I asked while hopping off the table and pointing at Esteban. "Shit, he's the one that shot you, so it's only right that you get your lick back."

"I thought you'd never ask." She smiled while pulling two Berettas from her back and sending bullets flying his way. In the blink of an eye, his life was gone. Camille was sitting next to him and was now dressed in his blood and brain matter. The moment that she noticed, a blood-curdling scream left her lips.

"Nah don't scream now mama! This is what you wanted. You didn't think that you could have gotten away with everything that you did, did you? You couldn't be that stupid!" I grabbed what I needed off the table and walked up to her. "Respect the game," I whispered in her ear while pushing the needle filled with fentanyl into her neck. Within a few short minutes, her screams faded, and silence filled the room as she took her last breath.

"So that's it? I thought this was gonna be a gruesome murder or some shit."

"Yeah, that's it. That allows her daddy to have an open casket funeral. Let's get out of here. I'm starving." The looks on Owen and Britton's faces were priceless. "Aye, the punishment fit at least one of the crimes, and I'm not a heartless bitch...yet." A smile graced my face, and it was so contagious that they smiled as well.

"Who gets hungry after they murder someone?" Britton asked Owen behind my back. I shrugged it off and jumped into the van. I was extremely happy that I was finally done with that situation.

51

SIX MONTHS LATER

ANI MACK

"Owen, we're going to be late if you don't hurry up!" I yelled up the stairs for Owen to come down.

Honestly, we should have been at the warehouse by now, but he was taking his sweet ass time. Two months ago, Owen officially moved into the house with me, while everyone else moved out. I had all of this space, and he was the best person to share it with.

"Calm down, why are you so nervous? You act like you don't know these people. This is your crew," he said while placing a kiss on my neck. To this day, whenever he touches me or even looks at me, chills down my spine.

"I'm not nervous, jackass. We just need to make a quick stop before we get there."

I had a surprise for him, and I was dying to show him what I'd done. If we didn't hurry, then he wouldn't be able to see all of it. He saw the excitement in my eyes and quickly grabbed the things that we needed for tonight.

"Where are the keys at?" I asked while pulling on the driver side door.

"What do you need the keys for? It's not like you're driving anywhere."

"Owen, give me the keys. You don't know where we're going, and I'm trying to surprise you. Let me have this moment. Please?" I batted my eyes at him in hopes that he would cave into my demands. He huffed and puffed, but eventually, he handed me the keys.

"Climb in and buckle up!"

"I knew this was a bad idea," he expressed while fastening his seat-belt and holding onto the door.

I don't know why he was doing all of that. He was acting as if I was a bad driver. I didn't have time to dwell on what Owen was trying to tell me with his body language. I revved the car up and put the pedal to the floor.

Thirty minutes later, we were pulling up to a large factory type warehouse. The look on Owen's face let me know that he had no clue why we were here. As I placed the car in park, a gentleman came out of the doors with a hard hat on and a smile. We had made it just in time. We both stepped out of the car and walked up to him.

"Hey, Ani. Nice to see you again!"

"Hey, Jamil. Thanks for coming out here today on such short notice. It's been a pain to hold in this secret, and I think it's time that I finally tell him."

"Okay, you guys ready?" Jamil yelled to the workers on the roof that held a cloth over a sign. The workers nodded and then the cloth fell. Big black shiny letters spelled out *Henry Pierce Training Academy*.

The night that Owen and I were at the lakefront, he expressed to me that he has a passion for security. He loved the uncertainty of each day, the thrill of the chase, and the satisfaction of protecting his client. He spoke about starting his own business, and after everything that we'd been through, I figured that it was the least I could do.

Owen came into my life, and he had been there for me since day one. There was no way that I could repay him for the things he'd endured. Let him tell it, that's the price of being Enticed by a Cartel Boss.

"Do you like it? Do you wanna take a look on the inside? Are you excited?" I fired off question after question hoping that he would answer just one of them. Instead of answering my question, he crouched down with his hands covering his mouth.

"Was this too much too soon? I'm sorry, Owen. I figured that it was something—"

"Calm down, baby. I'm just in shock. No one has ever done anything like this for me. Ma, this is truly dope. Thank you," he said while standing up and wrapping me in his warm embrace.

"Wanna take a look inside? It's not finished yet, but the contractor said that we're on schedule to be open in two weeks."

Jamil passed us two hard hats, and we walked the facilities with him. It was everything that I had envisioned for Owen, and he was absolutely impressed with it all. Unfortunately, we had to cut the visit short. The meeting that I had scheduled would be starting soon, and I refused to be late.

🐉

As I stood at the head of the table, I looked at the people before me. This family had been through it all these last few months, but we made it. Death was plenty, loyalty was tested, and relationships grew stronger. Without the people in front of me, I wouldn't have made it as far as I have.

After Camille's death, I received a phone call from Nikolas. He let me know that his time in the game had come to an end. He'd lost too much at the hands of his greed and disloyalty. He no longer wanted the lifestyle and had decided it was the right time to retire. Since there was no one for him to give his territory, he decided to pass it on to me. It came as a complete shock, and I wasn't sure that I was ready to handle more work. That's when I came up with a bright idea. I ran it past Kindred, and he was one hundred percent on board.

"I want to thank you all for everything that you all have done for me since I took over for Kindred." My father sat at the other end of the table with a smile on his face. "You've welcomed this newcomer and for the most things have been smooth. We've been through some shit—"

"Come on now. Don't draw out this speech and expect us to shed a few tears," Britton spoke up and caused laughter to fill the room. "We got parties to attend, ma'am. I'm tryna get white boy wasted."

"Yeah, you're right." I cleared my throat and got on with the purpose of this meeting. "As of today, the Edwards Cartel has acquired the De Lina Territory. With that being said, DJ, I'd like to hand over that territory to you. If you accept, you'll be able to run things your way."

A gasp escaped Britton's mouth and I could only imagine what was going through her head.

"Hell yeah, baby! That's amazing!" she squealed.

I let out a breath that I didn't know that I was holding. Brit and DJ had issues with his involvement in the game, and I knew that asking him would be a big risk. Seeing that Britton was excited about it was enough for me to end this meeting.

"Wifey has spoken. I'd be happy to accept, man. I appreciate it for real. Cali living here we come!"

"Okay now that the work has been done let's get the hell out of here and enjoy the weekend's festivities."

My parents finally decided to get it right and move forward with their relationship. Kindred wasn't letting Mariyah get away a second time. Tomorrow, they are getting married, and we have a whole weekend of partying to get to. I guess that Owen isn't the only one that was Enticed by a Cartel Boss.

THE END

ACKNOWLEDGMENTS

Wow, book number SIX! We've come so far since Perfect Dreams & Hood Nightmares. I cannot thank you all enough for rocking with me this far.

First and foremost, I want to thank the Lord for blessing me with this amazing talent. Never in my wildest dreams would I have thought that I would be here.

Mom, Jalisa, CJ, Destiny, Desiree, Keyana, and Maurice, thank you so much for your constant support. I appreciate everything that you all have done for me and will forever in debt to you.

Mz. Lady P, thank you for believing in me and giving me the chance to show my talents to the world. You believed in me and I'll continue to work hard to do you justice.

MLPP, y'all mean so much to me and you don't even know it. Special thanks to Yasauni, La'Nisha and my spirit sister Kyeate: When I wanted to quit, you all pushed me to the finish line, I couldn't have done this without your love, not so kind words, and support.

And to my readers, thank you for giving this little black girl from the south side of Chicago a chance to showcase her talents. The love and feedback has been overwhelming, and I thank you from the bottom of my heart.

Until next time.

Xoxo, Gavin

"Set your life on fire, seek those who fan your flames." -*Rumi*

OTHER TITLES FROM GAVIN

Perfect Dreams & Hood Nightmares: A Deadly Love Affair 1-3
Once Upon A Hood Love: A Miami Fairytale (Novella)
When Karma Comes to Collect Part 1

FOLLOW GAVIN VIA SOCIAL MEDIA

FACEBOOK: FACEBOOK.COM/ARIEL.GAVIN

IG: GavinTheAuthor

CPSIA information can be obtained
at www.ICGtesting.com
Printed in the USA
LVHW051934070519
616961LV00001B/151/P

9 781094 663050